BE
FRUITFUL
❧ & ❧
MULTI-*Lie*...

2-7-09

To Sibley.

God Bless You,

BE
FRUITFUL
&
MULTI-*Lie*...

PASTOR ROBERT E. WILSON II

TATE PUBLISHING & *Enterprises*

DEDICATION

First and foremost, I dedicate this book to my wife of seventeen years and the mother of our three children, Kimberly Alisa Wilson. You are the love of my life, my very best friend and have stood with me through the good times as well as the bad. You have taught me how to live, love and trust. Your strength has been my constant encouragement. May the blessings of the Lord continue to come upon you and overtake you as you continue to hearken unto His voice. You are my virtuous woman.

I also dedicate this book to our three children, Robert Edward III, Alisa Lanora, and Brandon James. Each of you are gifted, talented, smart and anointed for leadership and your gifts will make room for you. You all are the joy of my life, the sparkle in my eyes, and my reason for persevering. I love you and I am so very proud of you.

Finally, I dedicate this book to my parents, Robert E. Wilson I and Bettye Louise Wilson. Each of you is responsible for endowing me with love, wisdom, knowledge, intellect, dignity and self respect. I love you both.

ACKNOWLEDGMENTS

Absolutely none of this could be possible, had it not been for the Lord on my side. I thank God who created me, the Lord Jesus who saved me, and the Holy Spirit who comforts me. There were times in my life when I didn't understand why I had to experience certain things. However, as I was going through them and even after God brought me out, He revealed to me the necessity, that I might be made strong in Him.

Special thanks go out to every Pastor and every church that I have had the privilege of serving. I am certain that I have gotten out more than I had put in. Nevertheless, you've allowed me to grow and develop, hone and sharpen the gifts of God in my life and for this I am most grateful.

I also want to thank the entire staff of Tate Publishing. You have made this entire process so very easy and have been extremely supportive. Your unwillingness to compromise the Lord's standard for material gain along with your unwavering stance for holiness and righteousness is to be commended. Thank you and may the grace of God abound toward you all the more, that you might continue to have good success.

INTRODUCTION

'I wish I were a fly on the wall' or 'if I only had a bird's eye view.' These two common phrases that reference the arthropodous and ornithological kingdoms are rhetorical in nature but speak volumes for the scores of people who have an innate desire to be on the inside looking out rather than on the outside looking in. The reason either of these phrases are so frequently spoken or thought is because there is so much that goes on behind closed doors, behind the scenes and beneath the surface that the general public is not privy to, but somehow become the unsuspecting victims of... especially in the life of the local Black Baptist Church.

   Please don't get the wrong idea. This is not an attack on the local Black Baptist Church or the Baptist denomination at large. Neither is this a slanderous attempt to defame or demoralize any specific Pastor. This is however, *"Contemporary Christian Fiction"* written by one who just happened to be on the inside looking out. It is a novel, *inspired* by several different scenarios most of which have actually transpired over several years at several different churches. Although slightly enhanced through dramatic interpretation and compiled into one enlightening story, this easy read is long overdue. Subsequently, the names of the churches, the Pastors, and all involved have been changed. These pseudonyms are being used in an effort to draw more attention to the offense and not the offender, to the state of the universal church and not any one particular congregation. It is my heart's desire not only that the quality of the church be improved but also that the respect of the community be restored.

For me, it all started some thirty five years ago. I began attending a local Black Baptist Church in Brooklyn, New York, in the early 1970's. As a result, the gift of music was soon made manifest in my life. Excelling rapidly and becoming a child prodigy, soloist, pianist, organist, and choir director, they each served as precursors to a life and career as a Minister of Music, Minister of the Gospel, and current Pastor. However, prior to the Pastorate, I've had the privilege of serving at several prominent Baptist churches with several well known Pastors as their organist and or Minister of Music. This allowed me to be very close to all of the major action that went on behind the scenes and this myriad of experiences has prompted me to write this book.

I am in no wise attempting to assert my innocence in any of these matters, but I've taken full responsibility for the actions of my yesterday. I am fully persuaded that God has forgiven me, healed me, delivered me and set me free. Now I am living a life of liberty and peace, not carrying any guilt from the sins of my past. Not only that but I am committed to using the mistakes and experiences of my past to positively alter my future and promote a lifestyle of holiness in God's Kingdom here on earth.

Although there is no specific target group for this publication, as a young Pastor, I do have a special passion for young Ministers, and up and coming Pastors, who are very often mishandled, misled, misunderstood and following loyally but blindly. My objective is to awaken the spiritual senses of *all* who enter therein so that people learn not to get caught up in people. The manipulative philosophies and ideologies of some Pastors are powerful forces that covertly and overtly deflect people from trusting in an infallible God into trusting in fallible man. While they should be preaching and teaching the inerrant Word of God; their melodious monologues and pristinely polished sermons often reflect the thoughts, motives and intents of their hearts and not the heart of God.

The Apostle Paul lets us know that there is clear and present danger when we put our trust in men and not God. He writes in 1 Corinthians 2:1–5…

1. *And I, brethren, when I came to you, came not with excellency of speech or of wisdom, declaring unto you the testimony of God.*

2. *For I determined not to know any thing among you, save Jesus Christ, and him crucified.*

3. *And I was with you in weakness, and in fear, and in much trembling.*

4. *And my speech and my preaching was not with enticing words of man's wisdom, but in demonstration of the Spirit and of power:*

5. *That your faith should not stand in the wisdom of men, but in the power of God.*

You see, not only did I serve these leaders as a musician, but I served them in many other capacities. After all, I revered these men. I envied these men. I trusted these men. I wanted to be like these men. I served these men with my whole heart while putting God on the back burner. So, there was nothing that I wouldn't do for these men, who undoubtedly knew of my loyalty and willingness to do any and everything for them. I was their alibis and ran interference between them and their wives. I booked their hotel rooms, picked up and dropped off their women to them. I hand delivered the keys to their secret apartments to their other women. I picked up their liquor and for some was their personal pharmacologist. What was I thinking? The truth is that I was not thinking at all. I had some substance abuse problems of my own that clouded my perception and adversely influenced my judgment. I had put my trust in man and turned my back on God. Thank God for deliverance!

This eye opening saga prayerfully sheds some light on the impending presence of spiritual decay and the decline of the moral fiber and fabric that had previously been a badge of honor for the local church and its leadership. There was a time as recently as the 1970's, when the local church was at the forefront and center of everything that transpired in the community. In fact, everything that happened in the community came through the church whether it was social, economical, or political. The church and its leadership *were* iconic in the eyes of the community and in the hearts of the people... but things have changed. Somewhere along the way, the church and its leadership began displaying a form of godliness, but were denying the power thereof. Very simply, the church, *not God*, has lost its credibility in the community.

The respect, regard and high esteem that most people had for the local church and its leadership has significantly diminished based on knowledge of the actions of those in Pastoral and leadership positions. I could have written about the sporadically publicized, often minimized scandals that have of late rocked the Catholic Church, but that was not my experience. I pray for all of the individuals and families affected by the pedophiliac behavior of the fallen priests. I even pray for the priests, but personally speaking, that aspect of false religiosity masked by that level of inappropriate behavior is something that I cannot identify with.

I *can* only write about what I have experienced and what I have actually lived. I *can* write about the rarely publicized scandals that rock the local Baptist churches, and were quickly swept under the rug. Not surprisingly, because publicizing the idiosyncrasies of the Pastors and improprieties of the church would mean that the people who elected the Pastors and leaders would have been guilty of making a mistake in judgment. It would mean that those who have formed bonds and friendships with the Pastor and smiled in the Pastor's face and often expressed their approval for the job he was doing, would now have to publicly acknowledge their dissatisfaction. Not surprisingly, that rarely happened because the Pastor was a draw and really packed them in. So they let his little white lies slide and forgave his indiscretions.

They people concluded that as long as he keeps making us feel good, preaching us happy, and giving us what we want, we'll look the other way and pretend that things don't exist. They began to reason within themselves that he's really not doing anything more than what we ourselves are doing. It's called pardoning based on guilt. They even stay involved in the church. They stay connected to the church and yet they start talking among themselves, and on the telephone, and church becomes more of a social activity than a worship experience. The church continues to function but it is now devoid and destitute of the anointing and the power necessary to destroy the yokes of bondage.

The problem is that the ensuing result *is* fruitfulness. There is a whole lot of fruit being borne. Things are seemingly fruitful and prosperous and the church is growing and sprouting forth new generations but its new generations of Ministers and Pastors who have their father's spirit. That's part the allure. The fascination and attraction is being in leadership with all of its grandeur but not having to be accountable. Seeing this kind of misbehavior and being on the inside lets you know just how much you can get away with. For some of us, we were improperly groomed and mentored by our natural fathers as well as our spiritual fathers. Not only does the fruit not fall far from the tree, but according to the Word of God in *Matthew* 7:16 you are known by the fruit that you bear.

THE END...

DECLARING THE END FROM THE BEGINNING...
ISAIAH 46:10A

Ahhh! Sunday Morning! Listen! As the great hymn of the church Holy, Holy, Holy chimed from the belfry; it signaled that the eleven o'clock hour was drawing nigh. Not even the brutally cold, wintry weather of an early January day could stop the massive crowd of dedicated churchgoers from making their way into the house of the Lord. No single–digit wind chill factor, nor slush covered streets, nor ice slicked sidewalks could deter these determined faithful followers, passionate parishioners, oh, and let us not forget, church busybodies, from coming to find out what was really going on with their beloved Pastor. This newly renovated sanctuary with its lavish stained–glass windows was filled to capacity with approximately eight hundred congregants, including the balcony seating. Even with the main sanctuary filled to capacity, another seventy five latecomers worshipped via closed circuit television in the overflow room.

One would think that worshipping God *would* have

been their sole motivation or primary objective for pressing their way out to the church house under such inclem-
ent circumstances. The truth of the matter is that the
cloud of concern that hovered over them was so dense
that the thought of worship was being consumed by the
deceiving entanglement of the web of worry. What used
to be an enthusiastic entrance of an excited people with
their heads held high, has become a slow swagger of a
sorrowful, defeatist people with their heads hung low. Still
dressed to impress with their Sunday best, yet, no matter
how good they were looking on the outside, beneath the
surface something was indeed amiss. They knew exactly
what the Scriptures said in *Psalm* 100:4... *Enter into his
gates with thanksgiving, and into his courts with praise.*
That was their 'Call to Worship' every Sunday. However,
because of the circumstances their thanksgiving and praise
was being overshadowed by their (genuine) concern and
worry.

After all, this nationally renowned revivalist and
learned ecclesiastical prognosticator, the Right Reverend
Joseph M. Charles, III, the Senior Pastor of the illustri-
ous and prestigious Green Pastures Baptist Church for
over forty six years, had not mounted the pulpit in excess
of three months now. "I sure miss Rev. Charles' preaching," exclaimed Deaconess Campbell. "God knows that
man can preach. Don't get me wrong now. The associate
ministers have been doing a fine job and we have certainly
been blessed by the occasional guest pastors, but to me...
nobody can say it like good old Rev. Charles. He just
knows how to *move* me. Hallelujah! Thank you Jesus!"

The sentiments of Deaconess Campbell were consis-
tent with that of the majority of this Brooklyn, New York
based congregation. From the time Rev. Charles had taken

ill until now, things had just not been the same. There's been a certain feeling of emptiness and the church has been void of Pastoral leadership. Things were beginning to unravel and folks were starting to get uneasy. Amid all the special prayer meetings for the Pastor, private back-room meetings, three–way calls, presumptuous actions of a few overzealous associate ministers, and closed door clique conferences; with the exception of a select few, nobody really knew exactly what was going on with Rev. Charles and furthermore, what was going to happen to the church.

Under strict orders from Rev. Charles when he was still able to verbally communicate, First Lady Lula Mae Charles, their now grown–up children, John, Matthew, Miriam, their families, Deacon Willie Myers and I, had been instructed not to disclose the Pastor's condition and current status. Deacon Myers was the Chairman of the Deacon Board and longtime friend of the Pastor. I was the Minister of Music, Youth Minister and also like a son to the Pastor. The only thing everyone else knew was that Rev. Charles was very sick. What they didn't know was that he was gravely ill and knocking on death's door in the ICU of the Kings County Hospital. There were no visitors allowed except for the immediate family, Deacon Myers and me. Rev. Charles was even registered under a pseudonym so that the he would not be inundated with visitors and well wishers and the hospital overrun with flowers.

This was a far cry from the way everyone remembered Rev. Charles. The once very engaging, hands–on, people person with an infectious smile was now a mere shell of the man he used to be. Rev. Charles was a big man, not only in the upper echelon of preachers and in his reputation in the community, but he was also big in stature. Standing at six feet five and a half inches and weighing in at three hundred and fifty pounds, like most Baptist preachers he loved his share of fried chicken, macaroni and cheese, collard greens, and for dessert, homemade peach cobbler topped with Breyers Vanilla Bean ice cream. I can still hear Deaconess Campbell's voice echoing in the fellowship hall with her country accent saying, "That man sure could eat and he loved my peach cobbler. I used to tell him all the time that he didn't need it but he insisted that I make it for him. And "*whatsonever*" my Pastor wants, my Pastor gets." Needless to say, that was part of the problem.

Everybody knew he had high blood pressure and diabetes, but that didn't stop them from cooking him all of his favorite foods and desserts. All the while, the diseases and medications were taking their toll on his body. His heart and his kidneys suffered tremendous irreparable damage. He was going in and out of diabetic comas and passing out from hypoglycemic episodes. The effects of these diseases were rapidly progressing. That's what got him to this point. He's been bedridden for over three months, heavily medicated, experiencing rapid weight loss, and all of his vital organs are shutting down one by one. He was having trouble breathing on his own so they had him on a respirator. Looking at Rev. Charles was heartbreaking because he was hardly recognizable. I really didn't like seeing him like that. All of the members were pressing me for information, but I held fast to what the Pastor requested of me. However, all of the secrecy and knowing that something was wrong but not getting the whole story was really starting to affect the membership of the Green Pastures Baptist Church.

My guess is that part of the problem was that any other time, no matter what was happening, whether it was *bad news* or *good gossip,* it traveled fast and became the hot topic of conversation. Back then it wasn't hard to find out neither figure out what was going on. You remember the buzz when Pastor's middle son Matthew was strung out on crack and he robbed the Pastor's house. He stole Pastor's favorite gold cross and rope chain, all their other jewelry, his mother's fur coats and sold them so he could get high. Everybody had something to talk about. Especially when Matthew was trying to get clean and he got up and testified that the reason he was on drugs was because his father wasn't there for him and never spent any time with him. He had the nerve to say that his father was so busy being pastor and father to everybody else that he didn't have time to be a father to him. They talked about that for weeks but it soon lost its place to a series of unfortunate events surrounding Miriam, Pastor's baby girl.

Don't act like you don't remember. When little Miriam at sixteen years old popped up pregnant *after* receiving the Youth of the Year Award. After she made her acceptance speech, preached to all the other young people and declared how blessed she was to be living a holy life of abstinence and how she was saving herself for her Boaz, then 'ooops there it is!' Pastor and First Lady Lula were so embarrassed. Yet they held their heads up high and still supported Miriam and her son; their grandbaby. That didn't stop people from judging them and pointing the finger at them. That didn't stop people from talking. They still had stones to throw, like their glass houses were so squeaky clean. People are funny. Instead of praying for the Pastor and his family, they looked deeply and intently for Scriptures to ridicule that man. They won't read the Bible for the purpose of their own spiritual edification and eleva-tion, but they will read the Word to try to find something for their leader's spiritual assassination and degradation. You know what they said. They said stuff like, "The Bible says that if a man can't rule his own household, how can he manage the affairs of the church."

Pastor was a good man and a good father. He wasn't perfect, but that doesn't really matter because people are always going to have something to say. You know how church people are. They will always kick a man when he is down, instead of praying him up. It has been said that the army of the Lord is the only army where the soldiers will bury their wounded instead of trying to get them to safety, where they could be healed and restored. Yeah, I heard all of the things that were being said over the years but I didn't let any that stuff get to me. First of all, because I was on the inside looking out, secondly because I had problems of my own, and thirdly because Pastor was good to me. He was a mentor and a father to me when I didn't have anyone else. He gave me a chance when no one else would and I loved him with my whole heart. There was *nothing* I wouldn't do for him. *Absolutely nothing!*

Then it happened. The inevitable had come to pass. It was January 17, 2002 early one Tuesday morning, around 3:00 AM. My telephone rang and I knew that it wasn't good news. Wiping the sleep from my eyes I glanced over at the caller ID and saw that it was Deacon Myers. I hesi-tantly picked up the phone and said, "Hello." The voice one the other end, cracking and choked up said, "Well, Rev. Charles fought a good fight but now he's resting in the arms of Jesus. The Lord done called His faithful ser-vant home." I asked him, "Was anybody there with him?" He answered, "First Lady Lula and all the children were right there at his bedside. Sister Lula is the one that called me." I replied, "At least they were all there to say good-bye." I told Deacon Myers that I would speak to him later on that day, I prayed for the Pastor and his family, for the church family and then I cried myself to sleep knowing that weeping may endure for a night but joy would come in the morning.

The Announcement!

MOSES MY SERVANT IS DEAD...

JOSHUA 1:2A

The condition and status of Rev. Joseph Moses Charles, III could no longer be hidden. You know, most people didn't even know that his middle name was Moses. Although it was a Biblical name, Pastor was a little self conscious about it. Now, the secret was out and the cat was let out of the bag. Not only about his middle name, but news of Rev. Charles passing had begun to filter its way through some of the membership. My telephone was constantly ringing and the question of the day was, 'Is it true? Did Rev. Charles pass away?' Some of the choir members and a few of the musicians were blowing up my cell phone and they too had the same question. Everybody wanted to know if it was true. Did our beloved Pastor die, when did he die, and what did he die from? I couldn't even grieve properly because I was so busy answering everybody else's questions. It had gotten to the point where it was getting on my nerves, because the people with all of the questions and concerns now, were the same ones that were talking about the Pastor and his family.

Deacon Myers called me and said that he also was being bombarded with phone calls and it was beginning to stress him out also. I suggested that as Chairman of the Deacon Board, he take charge of the situation at hand. I told him that he should contact all of the servant leaders of the various ministries. Instruct them to contact all of their members and have the church clerk and secretary contact the rest of the membership for an emergency meeting on Wednesday evening at 7:00 pm. Thankfully, he heeded my suggestion. The calls were placed and all were duly informed of the meeting and told that it was business of importance.

As I pulled up to the church I could not hold back the tears that just seemed to flow automatically. I pondered for a few minutes before getting out of my car... that I would never hear another sermon from Rev. Joseph M. Charles, III again. Then I was comforted because I thought about the fact that it was because of one of his sermons I was moved to really give my heart and my life to the Lord Jesus Christ. I know his life was not lived in vain because the Lord used Rev. Charles to save me and to help turn my life around. With all of my many years growing up in church, hearing so many Pastors preach, playing behind them on the organ, Rev. Charles was the first Pastor that I actually started heeding. I heard a lot of sermons but I began to listen to Rev. Charles because of the passion he exemplified in delivering the Word. It just had a way of penetrating the very core of my heart. I'm sure going to miss Rev. Charles.

As I hesitantly got out of the car, I could hear the sounds of people wailing, crying and sobbing. Some were huddled in small groups embracing, while others were in circles of prayer. It was a pretty good turn out for it to be a last minute emergency meeting. There was at least eighty percent of the membership present. Nevertheless, the time was slipping away and Deacon Myers made his way to the microphone to call the house to order. He did so with a heart felt prayer for the Pastor that was so moving that if Rev. Charles wasn't in heaven already, that prayer sure would have put him there. He also prayed for the Pastor's wife, children and grandchildren, extended family, and the church family. He prayed that the legacy left behind by our Pastor would continue to grow and flourish and to that there was a rousing..."Amen!"

Deacon Myers then addressed the congregation and in his best efforts to contain his composure, he said these words, "Giving honor to God, who is the head of my life, to our Pastor in his absence..." He paused with his head down and with his eyes rolled up; he looked out among the people knowing he had just made a mistake. At the same time there was a collective gasp from the congregation as some just shook their heads in disbelief. Deacon Myers continued, "Giving honor to God, to all the ministers, deacons, deaconess, missionaries, officers, members and friends. It is with profound sorrow that I formally announce to you the passing of our beloved Rev. Joseph M. Charles, III. Rev. Charles passed away from complications brought on by sugar diabetes and high blood pressure and finally his heart just gave out. He made his transition early Tuesday at 3:00 in the morning with Sister Lula and the children at his bedside. I know that this is hard on us all because he was our Pastor, but let us please be mindful, considerate, and respectful and remember to pray for the family, because to them he was more than a Pastor. Amen?

I am so pleased by the turn out of so many of you tonight. We need each other and this is the time for us to pull together like never before. First Lady Lula and the children are handling the arrangements and the church is paying for everything. Rev. Charles left very specific instructions, however, everything else is our responsibility and we must make sure that we have everything in place. We don't want the family to have to worry about anything. Amen? Rev. Charles will lie in state beginning Sunday afternoon January 22, 2002 from 4:00 PM until 7:00 PM. People will be coming and going and during this time there will be a rotation of two deacons, deaconess or missionaries on either side of the casket for the remainder of all services. The family will be arriving at 6:45 and the wake service will be from 7:00 PM to 8:00 PM. At 8:00 there will be a musical celebration led by our Minister of Music whom you all know is like a son to Rev. Charles. It will consist of musicians and choirs worshipping God in song and in between songs there will be tributes given by the ministers, officers, servant leaders of each ministry, friends, family, and Pastors. We ask that all tributes be kept to a three minute minimum.

The funeral services, I mean the home–going celebration for our beloved Pastor will be on the following morning Monday January 23, 2002 at 11:00 AM. I expect every officer and member to be in their place and in the proper uniform. All clergy and ministers will be in their black robes. The deacons and all men will wear black suits with white shirts and white ties and the deaconess, missionaries and women will wear white dresses or white suits. Serving ushers with their badges and nurses with their badges and hats will be assigned to the family at all times. We want this celebration of life for our Pastor to be carried out in decency and in order. Not only do we have some food being catered, but everybody knows what it is that they are supposed to bring for the repast. We want to make sure we have enough food for everybody and we especially want to make sure that the family is fed first. Amen? I think that just about covers everything. Oh, just before we close, the James H. Thurgood Funeral Chapels is handling the body, but please send all floral arrangements here to the church.

I'm sure everyone has something to say, but if we start that, then we'll be here all night. Everyone is full of emotion and for this reason we are not going to open the floor up for questions or comments at this time. We know you all *love* the Pastor but let us show our love in our support and participation. If you have any questions, please see any one of the Deacons after the meeting. They will also have a printed outline of all the scheduled services. Faxes, calls, telegrams, e-mails, and even radio announcements, have been used to inform all of Pastor's friends, fellow Pastors, and the Christian community at large. Our secretary and the administration have been doing a wonderful job with the notification. I want to thank each of you so much for your time and consideration. Let us stand and be dismissed. May the Lord watch between me and thee, while we're absent, one from another, Amen!" As everyone prepared to leave out of the sanctuary, there was an awkward silence and you could hear everyone's foot steps as they shuffled through the pews on the hardwood floors onto the carpeted aisle. When they reached the vestibule, they all paused and glanced up at the portrait of Rev. Charles that hung with such pride. A picture is worth a thousand words...

The Home-Going

BLESSED ARE THE DEAD WHO DIE IN THE LORD FROM HENCE-
FORTH: YEA, SAITH THE SPIRIT, THAT THEY MAY REST FROM
THEIR LABOURS; AND THEIR WORKS DO FOLLOW THEM.
REVELATION 14:13

It was really a struggle getting through Sunday morning's worship service. It was just sad with a stifling tinge of morbidity. Everybody was physically there, but mentally and spiritually, everybody was somewhere else. There was such an overwhelming, heavy laden presence that the usual jovial worship service was reduced to that of a collective crying fest. As much as we tried to worship, all of our best efforts were overcome with grief. Knowing what was to come later that afternoon was too much to handle. So, the normal collective vocal responses of 'Amen' or 'Hallelujah' were hushed with occasional muffled cries and tearful outbursts of 'It's alright now' and 'thank you Jesus.' Nevertheless, the service moved along rather quickly and now it was time for the benediction. Usually after morning worship one of the ministries is serving dinners in the fellowship hall, but no one prepared dinners on this

Sunday. Some people went home to eat and then came back, while others settled for fast food or hero sandwiches from the corner bodega. Then there were those who didn't eat at all because they were too upset to eat. The time in between went rather swiftly and now it was time to get ready for what was to come.

I've never seen so many people in all my years of service here at the Green Pastures Baptist Church. From the time they laid Rev. Charles body out in the front of the sanctuary, all the way to the very last song sung at the musical tribute, the folks never stopped coming. The undertaker had changed the guest registry book five or six times. Rev. Charles sure touched the lives of a lot of people. I thought the reason most people came out on Sunday evening was because they had to go to work on Monday morning; but there seemed to be as many people there on Monday morning as there was Sunday evening. It's amazing how many lives Rev. Charles has impacted during his tenure here at Green Pastures. It was some home–going. I mean, it was really a home–going.

The way they had my Pastor laid out in that sky blue casket with gold trimming was something to see. That casket was the top of the line. I mean that thing was more luxurious than my car. It was the Cadillac of caskets and I know it cost a pretty penny. They sure had him dressed up nicely. He was decked out in his long white robe trimmed in gold, with gold buttons down the front and his favorite Bible in his hand. You know Rev. Charles only wore that robe a couple of times before he got sick. It was one of those new fancy robes. Rev. Charles sure looked good. His white hair was slicked back and wavy just like it always was. Yeah, he had lost some weight but Thurgood the mortician sure enough did a good job in making him look like himself. Pastor just looked like he was sleeping and you know, it was a peaceful kind of rest. There were so many moving moments at the services; I don't know which one I want to tell you about first.

Everyone was so tense and waiting with abated anticipation for the arrival of First Lady Lula, John, Matthew, Miriam, their families and the rest of the extended family. Although the sanctuary was full, with the exception of the reserved section for the family, there was still a massive crowd standing outside awaiting the arrival of the procession of limousines and personal cars. What a sight to see! There were six white, stretch limos, three Cadillacs and three Lincolns and at least a hundred cars behind them. There were cars for as far as the eye could see. There were so many cars that they had to have police escorts to control the traffic and not break the procession. Now you know you only get police escorts when you are down south. If you get a police escort up here in New York, then you must be somebody. My Pastor was somebody.

As the ushers cleared the front steps of the church and asked everyone to please go inside and be seated, most complied. But of course there were about two dozen people who just turned their heads, took a few steps back but remained on the outskirts of the entrance into the church. I guess they wanted to see what the family was wearing or how they were going to act when they got out of the car. You know there are some people who just love drama and some who are professional mourners. They only come to be nosey so they could have something to talk about. Much to their disappointment, the first family emerged from the limousines with an incredible degree of composure and dignity. The entire family was dressed in white and some of them had on dark shades, but their uniformity was an indication that as a family in the time of crisis, they united and came together like never before. The teachings of Rev. Charles were still speaking to us loudly and clearly through the exemplary behavior of his family.

First Lady Lula, the children and their families lined up two by two on the sidewalk and gracefully waited for the rest of the family to park their cars and join them in line. This of course took several minutes because there were so many, yet they all waited until each and every family member was in their place in line. As Rev. Charles was lying in state, everyone was walking around, talking and socializing but as soon as word got out that the family had arrived, people began to make their way to their seats and a hush fell upon the sanctuary. It was as if someone was presiding and had called the house to order. The only thing that could be heard was a faint sound of music playing. It was a mixed CD of all Rev. Charles' favorite songs being piped in through the house sound system.

The doors in the rear of the church had suddenly been propped open and First Lady Lula and Miriam were at the front of the line followed by John, Matthew and the rest of the family. With an incredible amount of strength and poise they processed in as Tramiane Hawkins', 'Going Up Yonder' played softly in the background. A slow and methodical walk down the long center aisle with their heads held high signaled to the waiting congregation that at least right now, at this moment in time, they had it all together. First Lady Lula and Miriam made their way to the casket, while John and Matthew halted the procession at the first pew.

First Lady and Miriam stood directly in front of Rev. Charles holding hands and wiping away tears. They paused for a moment and then First Lady stroked his wavy white hair and Miriam leaned in to give her daddy a good–bye kiss. John and Matthew then escorted them to their seats and then they stepped up to the casket. It was quite moving as the brothers comforted each other and bid their father farewell. John and Matthew remained standing and directed the rest of the family as they followed their example and upheld each other saying their good–byes two by two. Each child was accompanied by an adult and although this was a rather large family, with John and Matthew directing, the procession moved at a swift pace. This was truly grace under pressure.

The family had collectively decided that the actual home–going service would be a closed casket ceremony. So in essence, this wake and the musical tribute to follow was everyone's last opportunity to actually see Rev. Charles. What most people don't know was that there was a private viewing for the immediate family at the funeral home early Saturday evening. First Lady Lula, John, Matthew, Miriam and their families spent over two hours of private time with Rev. Charles. Most of that time was devoted to comforting the grandchildren. What the busybodies were expecting to see in terms of the family falling apart was done in private and the public services were done with impeccable class and self–respect. The frequent outburst and uncontrollable wailing and carrying on that was done while Rev. Charles was lying in state and even during wake was not done by the family. It was done by the church members. Some folk passed out and some folk had to be carried out. There were even some folk who were acting just down right ignorant but it was not a reflection on the family. They could not have given us a better example to follow.

There were two other memorable moments during this entire process that I want to share with you. One happened during the musical tribute and the other during the actual home–going service on Monday. The musical tribute was an awesome experience. It was full of worship and praise. The anointing was so high and the power of God moved mightily in the hearts of His people. Musicians and choirs from all over came to play and sing. Pastors and Bishops from near and far came to give tribute to Rev. Charles. The tributes were being done in between the songs. Since I was leading this worship service and was on the organ for most of it, I couldn't really see all of those who were coming to give tribute. I could see the Pastors and Bishops because they were speaking from the elevated pulpit. However, I could not see the lay people because they were on the other side of the sanctuary speaking from the podium down on the floor.

Everyone wanted to give tribute. All of the officers and those in leadership positions stood to say something on behalf of their ministries and their families. Of all the tributes given, one in particular stood out in my mind. A fellow by the name of Mark Houston stood to give tribute. I could not see Mark but I knew it was him because not only was he a member of Green Pastures but he also sang with the male chorus and I knew his voice. He had a distinct speaking voice that was easily recognizable.

Now, the only thing that was strange about Mark giving tribute was that he was not an officer or a ministry leader. He was not clergy or family. In fact, he rarely spoke in church at all. He was a faithful attendee, but not one who spoke publicly. Yet, his tribute was extremely heart felt and he was uncharacteristically overcome with emotion. I guess he loved his Pastor. The last thing that he said is what was so moving to me. He said, "If I had a father, I would have wanted my father to be just like Rev. Charles."

When Mark said that, he was so overwhelmed with grief that he nearly collapsed and had to be helped back to his seat by some smartly dressed woman, whom I did not recognize. Maybe it was because she wore a black hat with a veil. What a glorious musical celebration it was.

The home–going service on that Monday was indeed a celebration. The swelling amount of people that filled the church was a challenge to the ushers but with extra chairs down the aisles they managed to get everyone seated. There were so many dignitaries there that they were too numerous to name. There was representation from the Mayor's office and other state and local elected officials, yet everything ran smoothly and orderly. The service was presided over by one of Rev. Charles' best friends, the Rev. Clarence Norris, Pastor of the Ocean Park Baptist Church. The eulogy was delivered by Rev. Charles' very best friend, the Rev. Thomas Earl Williams. He is the very proud Pastor of the one of the fastest growing churches on the east coast, the New Jerusalem Baptist Church.

Rev. Williams did a great job eulogizing Rev. Charles and capturing the very essence of his life as husband, father, grandfather, Pastor, community leader and friend. Not surprisingly, there were a few tender moments and outward expressions of grief displayed by the family during the eulogy, but nothing that could even remotely be considered as tacky behavior. The same poise and dignity they displayed on Sunday at the wake and the musical was par for the course on Monday. The last memorable moment that caught my attention was the whimsical anecdote that Rev. Williams told during the eulogy.

He began to tell the story by saying, "You all know that Rev. Charles thought he was bad? No, I mean he really thought he was a tough guy because he was born and raised in the Bedford–Stuyvesant section of Brooklyn. He thought I was soft because I was from Bishopville, South Carolina and he always talked about how bad he was growing up in "Do or die, Bed–Stuy." Well, I want to let you all in on a little secret. Your Pastor was crazy and he carried a pistol. Well, he didn't actually carry it, but he kept it in his glove compartment. Now, he had a license to carry it and when he first got it many years ago, he used to go to the shooting range and keep it polished, but after a while it just sat in the car. I would ask him every now and then if it was still in there and he would say, 'Yeah man, it's in there somewhere.'

One day we were on our way to a meeting and we saw a little Puerto Rican boy snatch the pocketbook of this little old black sister, who looked like somebody's great–grandmother. She had just come out of the check cashing place. Well, Joe, I mean Rev. Charles got so mad that he turned beet red and said to me, 'Thomas, you see that.' I said, 'Yeah, I see it.' He said, 'Well, come on, let's do something about it.' Rev Charles threw that car into park, reached into the glove compartment and pulled out that old rusty gun and jumped out of the car. I jumped out with him because I didn't know what he was going to do. He told me to take out my wallet and act like I had a badge. So, we began to run after the little Puerto Rican guy. Rev. Charles pointed the gun and shouted, 'Freeze, it's the police!' Then he tripped on the sidewalk and the gun flew up in the air. The gun hit the ground and went off and both of us hit the deck. We were on the ground so fast that we didn't even see where the little Puerto Rican boy had gone. Rev. Charles scooped up that old rusty gun and we jumped back in the car two shades whiter than we were, breathing hard, scared to death and laughing our heads off."

The sanctuary was filled with needed thunderous laughter as Rev. Williams continued and stated that it was indeed a true story. That levity set the tone for the rest of the home–going service. And that same jovial spirit was even displayed at the cemetery. Everyone was focusing in on and remembering the good times. Sleep on now, Rev. Charles. Take your rest. We love you down here, but God loved you best.

THE BLESSED INSURANCE

A GOOD MAN LEAVETH AN INHERITANCE TO HIS CHIL-
DREN'S CHILDREN: AND THE WEALTH OF THE SINNER IS
LAID UP FOR THE JUST.

PROVERB 13:22

Now that the home–going services were finally completed, Deacon Myers, the chairman of the Deacons Board and Brother Oscar Jones, the chairman of the Trustee Board were in charge of making sure that the black and purple bunting was properly hung and displayed on the facade of the church. This symbol of mourning, tenderly prepared with the precision of a professional seamstress by Deaconess Susie Myers and the Deaconess Board, signaled to the community that our beloved Pastor had died. Since Deacon Myers and Brother Jones were both quite handy, not only did they see to it, but they pulled out the big rickety wooden ladder and actually hung the bunting themselves. While they were outside doing that the Deaconess' were inside draping Rev. Charles pulpit chair in a purple and black slipcover that fit to perfection. Both the bunting and the slipcover were to remain in place for a mourning period of one year. After that one year was past then there will be an unveiling service of Rev. Charles chair and the removal of the bunting; then and only then could the church even begin to entertain the calling of a new Pastor.

The Deacons, Trustees and the entire church were now eager to get back to the business at hand. Now that Rev. Charles was gone, what would become of the Green Pastures Baptist Church? So, exactly one week after Rev. Charles home–going service, Deacon Myers and Brother Jones called the Deacons and the Trustees together for a mandatory meeting; business of importance. The business at hand, very simply had to do with two insurance policies that the church had taken out on Rev. Charles. And by the way, these policies were already paid in full. Remember, Rev. Charles was the Pastor for 46 years and 46 years ago when they called him to be the Pastor, part of his benefit package was two $500,000.00 insurance policies. One of policies listed the church as the beneficiary and the other listed his wife and children as the beneficiaries. While the church paid for the policies, Rev. Charles did have complete control over the policies and he was personally in receipt of all correspondence from the insurance company.

The church *'religiously'* paid the premiums until each policy was paid off, but somewhere along the way Rev. Charles took out a loan against one of the policies to get his son Matthew out of jail. You remember when Matthew was out there and he got caught up in a drug bust. He was first time offender and a victim of the Rockefeller Drug Laws and they busted him with less than an ounce of cocaine and yet his bail was set extremely high at $100,000.00. Well, Pastor had to hire a lawyer to get the bail reduced and the lawyer and the bail had to be paid. So, Rev. Charles borrowed against one of the policies. It wasn't a secret or anything he was trying to hide. He told the Trustees what he needed to do. He informed them that he did not have the money at the time that his son got in trouble and in a timely fashion he paid back every cent of the loan. After all, Rev. Charles had complete control and authority over both policies.

Now, the church was not in any kind of financial difficulty; in fact they were quite well off. However, the existence of these policies was common knowledge. It was common knowledge that the family of Rev. Charles would benefit from one of the policies and the church would benefit from the other. This church was his life long work and although $500,000.00 is a lot of money; it by no means repays the family for the sacrifice they made in sharing their husband and father. Not only that but before Rev. Charles had become ill, he had just proposed the addition of a new educational wing. They had hired an architect to draw up plans, paid for the necessary permits, and had already secured a construction company. Surely, the proceeds from the other $500,000.00 insurance policy would help to bring Rev. Charles' vision into fruition. There was already some talk of naming the new educational facility the Rev. Joseph M. Charles, III Cultural and Educational Center. Nevertheless, the Deacons and the Trustees voted and agreed that this $500,000.00 bequeathment be used for the addition of the new educational wing.

Deacon Myers suggested to Brother Jones that he call a meeting with the Green Pastures Baptist Church Capital Improvement Committee, to thoroughly inform them of the half million dollar monetary bequeathment that would be earmarked for the new building project. Brother Jones

heeded the advice of Deacon Myers and called a meeting with the Capital Improvement Committee. One week
after the Deacons and the Trustees met, Brother Jones and
the committee met. Again, the existence of these policies
were common knowledge, but in this meeting the Capital
Improvement Committee was formerly told of the money
being earmarked for the new building project which they
were overseeing. Undoubtedly, this news was like music
to ears of the committee. Although they already had a
successful building fund plan in place, these additional
funds would speed up the process. The news of the entire
proceedings spread like wildflowers throughout the congregation and everyone was elated.

Ahhh! Good news for a change. People were talking
and they were actually talking about something positive.
Everyone was so excited about the news of the building
project going forward as well as the news of the inheritance that the church stood to receive. After collectively
dealing with the passing of their leader, this was the first
breath of fresh air allowing them to breathe a collective
sigh of relief. Something good was about to happen... but
could it happen without Pastoral leadership? Could the
vision come to pass without the visionary? The Bible says
in *Proverbs* 29.18...*Where there is no vision, the people perish.*
In this case the vision lives but the visionary has perished.
The vision has been written and made plain, but how then
shall they hear without a preacher?

It is said that a team without a coach will flounder. A
chicken with its head cut off, will run blindly and aimlessly
until it cannot run anymore. Likewise, a church without a
Pastor is like sheep without a shepherd. So, the people of
the Green Pastures Baptist Church being a proud people
thought that going forward with this building project

would be a testimony to their ability to function without a Pastor. They also genuinely believed that in doing this, they would be doing it in tribute to the teaching and leadership of Rev. Charles.

Their mode of thinking was that even though the church paid for the policy, after all Rev. Charles did for us, he was still blessing us even after he's gone. Rev. Charles is still making an indelible impact on the lives of the people he led for 46 years. The church was overjoyed at the idea of naming the new building the Rev. Joseph M. Charles, III Cultural and Educational Center. In doing so, his spiritual legacy would linger on. His family legacy would live on. His name would be carried on. And now, his financial legacy would increase the total net worth of the Green Pastures Baptist Church. First Lady Lula and their children were joint heirs of one policy. The members of the church were also joint heirs of the other policy, and not just heirs of the promise, but heirs of a total sum of $1,000,000.00.

The Discovery

A WISE SERVANT SHALL HAVE RULE OVER A SON THAT
CAUSETH SHAME, AND SHALL HAVE A PART OF THE
INHERITANCE AMONG THE BRETHREN.

PROVERBS 17:2

Things were progressing quite nicely and all of the pieces to the proverbial puzzle were beginning to fall into place. Except for the absence of Pastoral leadership, Green Pastures was really a fine tuned, well oiled machine that basically ran itself and it ran very smoothly and effectively because everyone knew their rolls. From the officers to the ministry leaders, from the administrator to the secretary, from the Minister of Music (that's me) to the sexton, everybody functioned within the confines of their specific assignments. There was an occasional ruffling of the feathers, an occasional misunderstanding, but if you've been a part of church as long as I have then you know that comes along with the territory. That's basic church stuff 101. When God starts blessing, that's when the devil starts messing.

The first family was trying their best to return to a life of quiet peace and a sense of normalcy. However, there was still a huge void and each of them in their own way was missing Rev. Charles tremendously. In the months of Sundays following the home–going, First Lady Lula, the children and the grandchildren each had difficult moments where they would break down during the worship services. They were not alone. Several members experienced tearful episodes of remembrance during worship, including myself. Every time someone got up to speak, they started off with the usual church greeting but added a new twist, "Giving honor to God, who is the head of my life, to the memory of my Pastor Rev. Charles, Deacons, Deaconess', officers, members and friends." Sometimes it evoked an emotional response and at other times it didn't affect us at all. I do know that First Lady Lula and the children were having their share of emotional struggles.

Although this was of no consolation, First Lady Lula, the children and the grandchildren did receive their inheritance. I know this first hand because Miriam and I are very close and she tells me everything. No, there's no funny business between Miriam and me, although she is kind of cute. She is only a couple of years older than me, but she is like a sister to me and I love her dearly. The way I understand it, out of the $500,000.00, First Lady and the children each received $100,000.00 and Miriam's son Ezra, Matthew's daughter Lydia, and John's two kids, Daniel and Rachel each received $25,000.00 in trust funds for their college education. If you do the math, then you realize that it adds up perfectly to $500,000.00. Rev. Charles was a great blessing to his now widowed wife, to his children and his children's children just like the Bible says.

Then it dawned on me that if the family received their inheritance, then the church should have received its inheritance as well. I hadn't heard anything up until this point, but I had figured that all was well and the money was where it was supposed to be. Later on that evening I got a telephone call from Deacon Myers. Deacon Myers only calls me when something is wrong. The phone rang and I answered it. "Hello," I said. Deacon Myers said, "Hey there, young fellow." I said, "What's up there, Deacon?" He said, "I think there is a problem with the money." I said, "A problem with what money?" He said, "You know what money, the insurance policy money." I asked him, "How do you know?" He said, "Brother Oscar Jones, the Chairman of the Trustees, called me and said we have a big, big problem with the insurance policy." I said, "What kind of problem?" He said, "I cannot talk to you about it over the telephone. We need to meet in person as soon as possible." I said, "Okay, that's fine Brother Jones. It's Friday night, so let's get together first thing in the morning over breakfast." He said, "Okay, that's fine. I'll see you in the morning over at Cora Bell's Country Kitchen at around 9:00 AM." Then I told Deacon Myers, "Well as soon as you find out what's going on with the money, then let me know and I'll talk to you tomorrow."

Cora Bell's is where they always ate breakfast. She serves the best country breakfast in town. She had everything you could possibly have imagined. Grits, eggs, hash browns, sage sausages, smoked sausages, mild and hot, slab bacon, liver pudding, pancakes, blueberry cobbler, waffles, preserves, homemade biscuits, and fresh squeezed orange juice. The truth be told, they both would have been there eating breakfast even if there was no meeting. They usually ate at the counter but were going to have to get a booth in the back, so that they could speak in private and not be interrupted. All night long I kept wondering what the problem was and trying to figure it out. I was overcome with eager anticipation and I couldn't sleep at all. The bottom line was that as intrigued as I was I still had to wait.

It was now 9:00 Saturday morning and Deacon Myers and Brother Jones were in Cora Bell's Country Kitchen eating their breakfast and discussing this big problem. Deacon Myers said to Brother Jones, "Alright Brother Jones, what's going on with the money?" Brother Jones said, "Well, Deacon Myers, you know that I am the Chairman of the Trustees and as Chairman I have been given power of attorney over the insurance policy and the inheritance that Rev. Charles left for the church. In other words, although the money is for the church, although the church is the beneficiary, I am the liaison, the contact person, the one that goes down to the insurance office and signs for the release of the check for $500,000.00." Deacon Myers said, "Yeah, yeah, I know all of that but what's the problem?"

Brother Jones continued, "Well, when I spoke to the agent on the phone about coming down to the office and signing for the release of the check, he informed me that I was mistaken and that the check had already been signed for and released. I told him that he was incorrect and that there was no possible way that anyone other than the Chairman of the Trustees could sign for that check and that I would be right there to settle the matter. When I got down to the insurance office I told the agent that maybe he was confusing the two policies and that First Lady Lula and the children had already received their checks from the first policy, but the church had not received their money from the second policy. I'm sure it's just a misunderstanding." "Well, what did he say," said Deacon Myers. Brother Jones replied, "He said that there had been a change in the beneficiary on the second policy authorized by Rev. Charles some ten years ago." Deacon Myers said, "What kind of change?" Brother Jones answered and said, "The agent said that he distinctly remembered that Rev. Charles came in about ten years ago and changed the beneficiary and told him that He was listing his son as the sole beneficiary of the second policy. In fact, he pulled up the paper work with Rev. Charles' signature authorizing the change."

Brother Jones said, "So I asked him which son was it, John or Matthew? And the agent answered and said, 'Neither one but Rev. Charles left specific orders that the identity of the new beneficiary not be released from this office. All I can tell you is that the young man about thirty something, who shall remain nameless, that came to sign for the check was overly adamant about who he was and how much he missed his father.'" Deacon Myers asked, "Brother Jones, what does this mean?" Brother Jones answered, "This means that we have a big, big, big problem. Not only is the church out of $500,000.00, but it seems like our beloved Rev. Charles has an illegitimate son of whom is now benefiting financially from the insurance policy that was paid for by the church and the proceeds designated for the church. Right up under our noses, good old Rev. Charles hid the fact that he fathered another child. What are we going to do and how are we going to handle this?"

Wow! As Deacon Myers was telling me all of this, my mind started racing, my heartbeat was increasing, my palms started sweating and I began to think about how this news was going to be delivered to First Lady Lula, John, Matthew and most of all, Miriam. I thought to myself that this could potentially have devastating repercussions for the family. Still coping with the loss of their esteemed patriarch, they will now learn that with all that Rev. Charles left behind, intertwined within that legacy is an illegitimate bastard son who by the way is now very well off. Well, this recent development certainly put a new spin on the Biblical phrase, "Be fruitful and multiply." In fact, we need to alter that phrase just a bit so that it is more befitting. It should be changed to, "Be fruitful and multi–lie." The truth of the matter is that there has been a whole lot of fruitfulness and that fruitfulness has been covered up by a multiplicity of lies and deceit.

THE SECRET IS OUT...

FOR THERE IS NOTHING COVERED, THAT WILL NOT BE
REVEALED; OR HID, THAT SHALL NOT BE KNOWN.
MATTHEW 10:26

At this point in time, Deacon Myers, Brother Jones and I are the only ones who are aware of the alleged misadventures of Rev. Charles. Deacon Myers informed Brother Jones that he had been confiding in me because of my relationship with Rev. Charles and the family. We all agreed that this potentially earth shattering discovery must be handled very delicately and not yet made public knowledge. I certainly had not discussed these matters with anyone and Deacon Myers and Brother Jones hadn't even told their wives yet, fearing that if this was noised abroad incorrectly, it could destroy the church. Not that they didn't trust their wives, but they decided to pray about it first even before bringing it to their wives. Quiet as it's kept, Deaconess Susie Myers and her prayer partner Missionary Ophelia Jones, who was Brother Jones' wife, did more than just pray on the 'hellephone,' I mean telephone.

Eventually, Deacon Myers told his wife, Brother Jones told his wife and I called my mother and told her. Now there were six people who actually knew what had taken place. It was asked of the latter three that were informed that they keep the information strictly confidential until a formal meeting with the Deacons and the Trustees. That meeting would soon be followed up by a meeting with the entire congregation. The reason we asked them to keep it hush-hush was to protect and shield First Lady Lula and family. We did not want to leave the door open for the congregation to speculate and spread all kinds of rumors and falsehoods. The situation was critical enough in and of itself and it certainly did not require any additional unfounded spins on top of it.

In the announcements on the following Sunday morning, the Deacons and the Trustees were asked to report to the church conference room on Monday at 7:00 PM—business of major importance. While it was up to Deacon Myers and Brother Jones to inform the Deacons and Trustees, I was left with the task of informing the First Lady Lula and the family. I was betwixt and between as to how I would actually do it; whether I would address First Lady by herself or Miriam by herself, since we were so close. Then I began thinking that maybe this was something that the brothers, the men, John and Matthew would be able to handle better and then they would share the news with their mother and sister. I was totally confused and at a loss as what I was going to do, so I decided to get all of them together and tell them at the same time. One thing that I knew I had to do was tell the family at the very same time Deacon Myers and Brother Jones were telling the Deacons and the Trustees... for obvious reasons. They did not deserve to hear news of this magnitude through the grapevine or be subject to the spiteful haters who would call or visit, and add their two cents just to pour salt in the wounds.

It was now Monday evening at approximately 6:55PM. John, Matthew and I pulled up to the Charles family driveway at the same time. Exiting our vehicles I tried to maintain a stoic unreadable face, while John's and Matthew's expressions were that of concern and perplexity. As we walked up to the front door, John was looking for his keys to let us in. Both John and Matthew have their own homes, but they kept a spare key to the home that they grew up in to check on their mom and the house. Matthew stated that his key was back at his house and he hadn't carried it in a good while.

So, we entered the house and went directly into the den where First Lady Lula had tea, coffee, cookies and doughnuts set up for us. Of course we went straight for the goodies as Miriam was wiping the sugar from the powdered doughnuts from her mouth. I said jokingly, "What's the matter Miriam, you couldn't wait for us?" She replied, "The Bible says wait on the Lord not yawl and it also says that if any man hunger let him eat at home." There was a chorus of laughter that abruptly ended with a collective sigh.

John spoke up and said, "Okay, let's get down to business. Why are we here? The message that you left on my voice mail said that it was vitally important. So spit it out. Wait, don't tell me. You got a better offer as Minister of Music at another church?" I replied, "No, that's not it." Matthew said, "You're getting married?" I said, "I wish I was." Miriam chimed in, "You're not getting ready to come out of the closet, are you?" I firmly responded with a little more added bass in my voice, "Why of course not.

Don't be ridiculous. However, there are some things that are coming out of the closet and they are in the form of a few skeletons."

"Boy, what in heaven's name are you talking about?" said First Lady Lula. I said, "As you all know there is a meeting of the Deacons and the Trustees going on right now." "Yeah, we know, we know. What does that have to do with us?" said Matthew. I answered with as serious a face as I could have put on and I told them, "Everyone please sit down because this is not going to be easy. The meeting that is going on right now at the church is to inform the Deacons and the Trustees that there was a major problem with the other insurance policy that the church had out on Rev. Charles."

"What kind of problem? Was there a lapse in the policy and the policy not valid? We didn't have any problems at all with ours," said First Lady. I answered, "Well, when Brother Jones, the Chairmen of the Trustees called the insurance broker to tell him he was coming down to pick up the $500,000.00 check for the church, the broker told him that there was some kind of mistake because the check had already been picked up." John responded, "I'm sure that's a common mistake in their business. One of the other Trustees must have picked up the check earlier." I replied, "I wish it was that simple, but it is not. It turns out that about ten years ago, Rev. Charles amended that particular policy and changed the beneficiary from the church to someone else."

"What somebody else!" shouted Miriam? I said, "Well, it turns out that the insurance company was told that they could never reveal to anyone who it was but they did tell us that the check for $500,000.00 was picked up by a young man in his mid–thirties who adamantly declared that Rev. Charles was his father." First Lady cried out, "What are you saying?" I answered, "What I am saying is that the $500,000.00 inheritance that the Green Pastures Baptist Church was expecting to receive, being that they paid on the policy for all these years, was picked up by an anonymous young man who said that Rev. Charles was his father. I'm sorry to be the bearer of such bad news but it seems Rev. Charles had another son, whom he decided should be the sole beneficiary of the other policy."

Miriam cried in defense of her father saying, "Another son? This must all be a terrible mistake. My daddy wouldn't do that. Not my daddy. This is a hoax and somebody is attempting to rip the church off of the $500,000.00. Did anybody call the police?" I replied, "No, the police were not called. If the insurance company thought for one second that there was foul play involved, there is no way they would have released a check for that amount to the young man. In fact, they pulled up the records of when Rev. Charles went in and amended the policy and the broker told me that the valid identification and valid social security card that the beneficiary presented was an exact match to what Rev. Charles had put down on the policy."

Everyone sat back for a few minutes and tried to digest what they had just been fed. First Lady Lula broke down, fell on her knees and began to weep uncontrollably. Matthew ran to hold and comfort his mother while tears ran down his angry face. John was pacing back and forth, shaking his head from side to side and saying, 'no, no, no' over and over again. Miriam took off running and went upstairs to the bedroom of her sleeping son Ezra. She kneeled at his bedside and cried like she had never cried before, yet with a pillow she was trying to muffle her outcry so as not to awaken the sleeping innocence. Fearing she would startle Ezra, Miriam soon left the room and ran back downstairs to be with her mother.

As they all wept, the thunderous, roaring, angry voice of John declared, "I'm going to find out who this is if it's the last thing I do!" I felt the need to keep apologizing to them all and I was really trying my best to comfort them, but it was to no avail. Matthew and Miriam escorted First Lady Lula to her bedroom, got her some aspirin and water and put her in the bed. John stormed out of the house and screeched his tires as he peeled out of the driveway. I bid them all good night and sat in my car and cried for about fifteen minutes before I was able to drive away. The pressure of being the messenger of such a damaging revelation to a family I care about was heartbreaking and I could no longer contain myself.

While proceeding to pull off, my cell phone rang and it was Deacon Myers. I asked, "How did it go Deac?" He answered, "It didn't go too well. Everybody broke down and there were so many questions. Some of them Negroes even accused me and Brother Jones of conspiring to set up a nest egg for ourselves." I said, "You're kidding me?" Deacon Myers said, "No, I'm not kidding! Those Deacons and Trustees seemed to be more upset about the $500,000.00 then they were about the fact that Rev. Charles had a bastard son." Deacon Myers then asked, "Well, how did it go with the family?" I said, "To tell you the truth Deac, I have never seen them so broken before. I have been a part of this family for almost twenty years and I have never seen this kind of pain before. They are going to need much prayer and healing. My mother always said, 'If it doesn't come out in the wash, it will come out in the rinse.'"

The Aftermath

A MERRY HEART MAKETH A CHEERFUL COUNTENANCE:
BUT BY SORROW OF THE HEART THE SPIRIT IS BROKEN.
PROVERBS 15:13

Well, needless to say, before Deacon Myers and Brother Jones could call a meeting of the entire congregation to disclose the totality of the situation, somehow everyone already had knowledge of what had transpired. In a matter of six days, it went from six people knowing, to me informing the family and the rest of the Deacons and Trustees finding out in a meeting. I'm quite sure it wasn't the family that was doing the talking, although John and Matthew did tell their wives. Somebody else must have been doing some serious talking among the Deacons and Trustees and then they told two friends, and they told two friends and so on and so on and so on... Almost instantaneously, it jumped from a few people knowing to more than a thousand people knowing. I'm telling you that by the time Sunday came, everybody and their grandmother knew. I sure wished that the *Good News* traveled that fast.

While there were quite a few loyal and spiritual folks

who earnestly sympathized with and prayed for the family, the vast majority of people were mainly concerned about the money. They all began chiding, 'What happened to the money? I knew something wasn't right! There aint no child, somebody's trying to pull a fast one!' Not only that, but those same folk now speaking out of the other side of their faces, also wanted to know who this mystery child was; although he technically was not a child anymore. This person, whoever he was, was a grown man and the people wanted to know who he was. In addition to that, as if that wasn't enough, they also picked their moments to take pot shots at the late Rev. Charles. They kept making reference to the fact that good old Rev. Charles had an illegitimate, bastard child outside of the bonds of his holy matrimony. They also alluded to the fact that Rev. Charles stepped out on First Lady Lula.

The tension in the air was so thick that following Sunday, you could have cut it with a knife. Worship was almost impossible because the preoccupation with the current events reduced the service to a quiet walkthrough of ceremonialism and tradition. Getting into the flow of worship was not an option because the atmosphere was so charged with the full gambit of emotions that no one was really paying attention to what was going on. As I sat on the organ and took a panoramic view of the congregation, I saw some people with their heads down, some with their heads in their hands, some staring straight ahead, some looking up, some with their eyes closed, some with tears in the wells of their eyes, some embracing others, some stoic, while others displayed looks of disgust, anger, bitterness and resentment. There was literally (as the Bible says) weeping and gnashing of teeth.

The J. M. Charles Sanctuary Choir attempted to lead

the church in the sermonic hymn but it was more like a choir selection because no one in the congregation was singing along. When the choir finished there were a few scattered Amens, but I had a cartoon moment and all I heard were crickets chirping. I certainly did not envy the one who was to stand and preach on this Sunday morning. You won't believe who was preaching. It was the Assistant to the Pastor, Rev. Andrew Jefferson. He was an old fashioned, fire and brimstone preacher and when most people knew ahead of time that he was preaching, they chose that particular Sunday to go visit other churches. Not me. I kind of like Rev. Jefferson's style. Yes, he was missing a few teeth and was a tad bit dogmatic, but he sure could sing and I loved playing the organ for him.

Rev. Jefferson sure had his work cut out for him. He started out by saying, "If we've ever needed the Lord before, we sure do need him now!" To this statement there was a varied response. Some shouted, 'Amen!' While others shouted, 'We need you Lord!' Still others shouted, 'Right now, right now!' For Rev. Jefferson that was more of a response than he was used to getting. I think it gave him confidence, because he seemed to perk up and talk with more passion in his inflections. Not only was he the senior minister within the church in terms of experience, but he also surpassed everyone else in terms of longevity at Green Pastures.

As he began preaching he said, "I prayed and asked the Lord what He would have me to say to you during these troubled times. I was being led in several directions. First I thought I would preach from the subject, 'People In Glass Houses' with *John* 8:7 as the text. You know that's the Scripture about the woman caught in adultery *with the man* that says, 'He that is without sin among you, let him first cast a stone *at her*. I wasn't quite settled on that and then I was thinking about preaching from the subject, 'Clean Up Your Own Backyard' with *Matthew* 7:1–5 as the text. You know that Scripture about the beam and the mote. First cast the beam out of your own eye and then you can see clearly to cast the mote out of your brother's eye. That wasn't the one either.

Then I began reading the Word some more and I turned to *Galatians* 6:1, where it talks about a man being overtaken in a fault and those who are spiritual restoring him with the spirit of meekness, lest they also be tempted. I was going to use as a subject, 'I Thought It Couldn't Happen to Me.' That wasn't it either. Then the Lord spoke to me definitively and told me that the only way healing was going to come in this house was if everybody learned to truly forgive. From the Pastor's family to the entire church family, healing would come as a result of our being able to forgive. So I want to use as a subject, 'The Danger Of Expecting What You're Not Willing To Give.'" Rev. Jefferson went on preaching and said, "Learning to forgive takes some time but it also requires some effort on our behalf. We do not master it overnight, but in the process we cannot allow unforgiveness to master us."

Now I have heard Rev. Jefferson preach on many occasions, but to be honest, he had gotten off to a better start this time than ever before. It seemed as if God had suddenly endowed him with great wisdom because everything that he was saying was so deep. Maybe just maybe that was the way he always preached but because of our preconceived notions, judgmental comparisons, and our preaching preferences, we subconsciously tuned him out and didn't give him a chance. *Not!* This time he really hit the nail on the head. His message was certainly timely and needed as the church collectively and individually dealt the aftermath of Rev. Charles passing as well as the unfortunate incidents following.

Old Rev. Jefferson was winding up his sermon now. He was bringing it on home and he tuned up just like an old Baptist preacher. I was with him every step of the way backing him up with those real churchy preaching chords. Suddenly there were signs of life within the congregation. A few people stood up and got right with Rev. Jefferson. It wasn't the usual celebratory climax that happens toward the end of a sermon, but it was much livelier than the earlier parts of the service. Then Rev. Jefferson said these profound words, "As I prepare to take my seat, I want to leave you with this. Unforgiveness never really hurts the one in need of forgiveness. Life is funny and as life would have it, you may never get the chance to actually tell the offender that you forgive him or her, but in your heart whether you get to tell them or not, you must forgive for Christ's sake and for your own sake. There is grave danger in expecting what you are not willing to give. Let the church say Amen!"

Rev. Jefferson then opened the doors of the church and gave the invitation to Christian Discipleship. Then he sang the song that I hoped he would sing because I loved playing for him. Did I say that I loved playing for him? He sang, "I shall forever lift mine eyes to Calvary, to view the cross where Jesus died for me. How marvelous, that grace that caught my falling soul. He looked, He looked, He looked beyond my faults and saw my needs."

The Search Begins...

GO AND SEARCH DILIGENTLY FOR THE YOUNG CHILD; AND
WHEN YE HAVE FOUND HIM, BRING ME WORD AGAIN...
MATTHEW 2:8

I was really trying to get a general consensus as to how everyone was processing everything that went down. Aside from everyone's demeanor and how their outward manifestations of frustration were easily read, I needed to know how they were doing on the inside. How were they internally dealing with the fact that Rev. Charles single–handedly orchestrated the changing of the beneficiary on the insurance policy? How were they feeling in their hearts about giving to the church when the church unknowingly allowed what amounts to be a misappropriation of funds? Was the church going to be in financial trouble, now that this money that was figured into the new building project, didn't exist? From speaking with quite a few people, these concerns were indeed at the forefront of everyone's mind, but there was one issue that seemed to be more paramount. There was one unsolved mystery that had taken precedence over the $500,000.00.

It was the issue of the newly discovered son that was pressing on the hearts and minds of the people. Everyone wanted to know who this young man was and also who his mother was. Who was this mystery woman that Rev. Charles, not only cheated on his wife with, but also conceived a child with? I don't mean to speculate but she obviously knew that he was a Pastor and was married with children. Rev. Charles was nationally known and somewhat of a celebrity personality in this area. Who didn't know Rev. and *Mrs.* Charles?

Huh! As fine as First Lady Lula was, this other woman had to have been a dime piece. Now, I have seen some of Rev. Charles' other friends, and I have taxied a few of them here and there. In fact, I have personally chauffeured some of them to their secret rendezvous points and I must admit that they were definitely something to look at. Rev. Charles kind of took me under his wing and was schooling me but every now and then he would jokingly say to me, "Boy, you can look; but this one right here, you better not touch." This particular incident with this woman happened before my watch, but judging from his taste, she must have been drop dead gorgeous too.

A couple of weeks had gone by since I first met with the family and was the bearer of bad news and the messenger of misfortune. We were now going to meet again, but this time they called the meeting. My phone rang and it was John on the line and he asked that I meet with him and the rest of the family back at the Charles family home. Now, I didn't call this meeting, so naturally I was a little curious as to what we would be meeting about. To tell you the truth, I was just glad to be included; glad to be considered as one of the family. The meeting was scheduled for Monday evening at 7:00 PM.

This time when I pulled up to the house, I could see by the cars parked outside that everyone else was already inside. I thought to myself, maybe they had a meeting before the meeting and now were awaiting my arrival. After this deduction, all kinds of things began to run through my mind. I began thinking that maybe they thought that I was Rev. Charles illegitimate son. Maybe because of the relationship that Rev. Charles and I had, they suspect me of being in receipt of the $500,000.00. I did just purchase me a brand new Lincoln Navigator, but I worked hard for that. Yes, I put down a substantial down payment but I still have a car note.

No, that's just crazy. They can't possibly think that it's me. Can they? I do fit the bill. I am in my mid–thirties, okay late thirties and people have said that I look like I'm part of the family. I have been mistaken for Rev. Charles' son before. I did know more information about this situation than any of them. Okay, okay... Let me clear my mind and stop the madness. I can't believe that from the time it took me to get out of my car and walk up to the front door, all those thoughts entered my mind. They say that an idle mind is the devil's workshop but my mind wasn't idle for very long. The devil was just trying to stir up some mess.

I reached out to ring the bell but before the tip of my finger could touch the bell, the door swung open and I was invited in very sternly by John. He pretty much ushered me into the den, but this time there was no tea, coffee, cookies and doughnuts. I felt all eyes on me and as I greeted each of them, I was not met with the usual enthusiasm. In fact, it seemed that everyone was a bit reserved and standoffish. I started to think to myself, 'Maybe they really do think that I'm the son.' With this in mind, I engaged them and asked, "All right, what's this meeting about?" John almost interrupting me said, "I think we should be the ones asking the questions." I immediately responded and speaking as quickly as possible said, "I don't know what you all are thinking, but I am not Rev. Charles' son. I don't have the insurance money. I bought my car with my own hard earned money. I know who my father is and I would never do something like that to you all."

They all looked at each other and then looked back at me. There was a momentary eerie silence that was soon interrupted with a hysterical outburst of laughter. First Lady Lula, John, Matthew, and Miriam were overcome with great amusement at my expense. John still laughing managed to squeeze out, "Is that what you thought this meeting was about?" Then Matthew said, "Man, you must be losing it." Miriam joined the bandwagon and said, "You have always been our brother from another mother, but we didn't think that you thought that we thought it was you." Finally First Lady Lula remarked, "Well, now I done heard it all. That's not why we called you here, baby." I asked, "Well, if that's not why I'm here then why were you all acting so funny?"

John answered, "We were feeling a little strange because we do have some questions for you, and we didn't know exactly how to ask them. We didn't want to offend you in any way. We obviously know how close you were with our Father. We know of your loyalty and devotion to him." Then Matthew continued, "Listen, we are all adults here and we know that although the Right Rev. Charles was a great provider, a good father and a good Pastor, we all, *including* my mother, knew that he was very fond of the ladies and the ladies were very fond of him." Miriam interjected also, "We are not asking you to betray our father, but we do know that you were his inside man. We do know that you were a lot closer to the action than anyone else. We know that you were a friend to the Pastor. We just wanted to know, if it is at all possible, you might have some information as to who this person is who is supposed to be our half brother."

First Lady Lula then said in her usual sweet tone of voice, "Now, before you answer, please be well assured that no matter what happens we will keep your name out of it. Rev. Charles loved you and we know you loved him too. But, if you have anything, if you know anything that will help shed some light on who this child or should I say man is, it will be deeply appreciated." Feeling relieved that they didn't think it was me, I answered, "It is true that I know a lot more of Rev. Charles' personal business than most. It is also true that I was privy to some things concerning Rev. Charles that I am not particularly proud of, but in this case, in this instance I know absolutely nothing."

I told them, "This was a surprise and shock to me as well and if I knew anything I would gladly fill you in. Remember, I've only been minister of music for close to twenty years. This son was born long before I started at Green Pastures. This was indeed Rev. Charles best kept secret. Let me ask you a question. Do you think that this son has ever been to Green Pastures Baptist Church?" John answered, "No, he couldn't have. I know daddy was crazy but he wasn't that crazy." Then First Lady Lula said, "I don't know. You can't put nothing past him now. Maybe the boy did visit Green Pastures every now and again." I then advised them, "You probably need to converse with a few of the old timers. You know the ones who were there when Rev. Charles first got called to the church. If the insurance man was accurate in his assumption about the age of the young man being in his mid–thirties, then that young man is either a couple of years older than you Miriam, or a couple of years younger. Nevertheless, before I came on board, Rev. Charles must have been close to somebody else or confided in somebody else."

John then said, "That makes a whole lot of sense. See, even though you didn't dish out the goods on dear old dad, you still came through in a big way. We just have to put our heads together and think back as to who was close to daddy during that time. Mommy, since we were quite young, I think you are going to have to help us with this." Then First Lady Lula said, "I will help you as much as I can, the Lord be my strength. Now, I will tell you this, children, while we search for the truth, you all need to prepare yourselves to hear things about your father that you have never heard before. Some true and some not true. You see, anytime you move the rug that dirt has been swept under for so many years, you are subject to find some old dirt that was covered up that might have been better left covered."

The Search Continues...

NOTWITHSTANDING I HAVE A FEW THINGS AGAINST
THEE, BECAUSE THOU SUFFEREST THAT WOMAN JEZEBEL,
WHICH CALLETH HERSELF A PROPHETESS, TO TEACH
AND TO SEDUCE MY SERVANTS TO COMMIT FORNICATION.
REVELATION 2:20

After advising First Lady Lula and the children to talk
with a few of the long time members and possibly those
who were at one time or another very close to Rev. Charles,
it dawned on me that I already had direct access to Rev.
Charles right hand man. Deacon Myers, the resident his-
torian, was the Chairman of the Deacons for the entire
duration of Rev. Charles tenure as Pastor. He was Rev.
Charles' ace boon coon. Although Deacon Myers denied
knowing anything about the change in the insurance policy's beneficiary and denied having any knowledge of Rev.
Charles' illegitimate son, I was sure he had some pertinent
information that he might have unconsciously been stor-
ing in the innermost recesses of his mind. It was time for
me and Deacon Myers to have a little sit down. I figured
that by speaking to Deacon Myers in depth, he might be

able to share some incidents from the past that could perhaps give me some insight on the identity of this newest addition to the Charles family. Somebody has to know something.

I knew that Rev. Charles had a history before I got to Green Pastures, but as far as I was concerned not only was it 'his—story' but it was the past. After all, he was still the Pastor, so whatever it was, it must not have been that bad or the congregation simply excused and or forgave his behavior. It was either that or only a select few new the real deal. What I have found out is that some church folk will put up with anything as long as their authority is not challenged. They will even allow the Pastor to do whatever he is big enough and bad enough to do, as long as he keeps the people coming. Rev. Charles was definitely guilty of keeping the people coming. From the time I started as Minister of Music, the preaching style and charismatic appeal of Rev. Charles, the man, coupled together with an occasional anointed Word from Rev. Charles, the preacher, caused the membership as well as the offerings of Green Pastures to increase annually. In turn, the church took very good care of Rev. Charles. Now, with all of the good that Rev. Charles had done, I have a feeling that when we get to the bottom of this particular issue, this might be what he's remembered for most.

I called Deacon Myers and told him I was coming over to talk with him and Deaconess Susie Myers. I strategically and purposefully included his wife because now that everything was common knowledge, I figured that including her would be to my advantage. She was very well known for keeping up with everything that went on in and around the church. She was the resident busybody. Let's just come right out and say she was the nosiest, busiest, gossip in Green Pastures. Even though Deacon Myers was Rev. Charles' right hand man, I was convinced that Deaconess Susie Myers was sitting on much more information about Rev. Charles than Deacon Myers had even known or was even concerned about.

I went over to the Myers' residence, broke bread with them and then we moved to the sitting room where we began to engage in conversation about the ordeal in its entirety. I started out by saying, "Deacon and Deaconess Myers, as far as I know and based on what I have been told, the two of you were at Green Pastures when Rev. Charles was first called to be Pastor." They both responded in stereo, "Yes, that's right!" I continued, "First Lady Lula, John, Matthew, and Miriam have asked me to help them find out not only who this young man is, but also who his mother is. I figured that since you all were there since the beginning; there might be something that you remember; some specific incident that might tie in. I don't mean to be presumptuous, but based on the fact that the two of you were serving as Deacon and Deaconess from the inception of Rev. Charles' service at Green Pastures, I reasoned that if there is something that might help, then you two would have the answers.

So I want to begin by asking you, is any one thing that you can recall from an earlier time that could remotely be tied into the mess that is going on now? Do you remember any inappropriate relationships that Rev. Charles may have had? Do you specifically remember who was sweet on Rev. Charles back in the day?" Deacon Myers answered, "Well, to tell you the truth, there were a whole lot of women that were after Rev. Charles but he didn't keep time with all of them." Then Deaconess Myers jumped in and said, "No, he didn't keep time with all of them but he sure kept time with enough of them. I used to feel so sorry for Lula Mae. I know she saw all of those Jezebels up in Rev. Charles' face, and He was just a grinning. Those women just didn't have any respect for the First Lady nor their marriage. And Rev. Charles didn't help the situation much."

Deacon Myers then asked, "Susie, what in heavens name are you talking about? Rev. Charles was good to First Lady Lula." She snapped back, "He may have been good to her but all that flirting and messing around that was going on right up under her nose was not good for her. I don't care what you say." I thought to myself, 'Now we're getting somewhere.' I asked, "What flirting and what messing around? I'm taking names and numbers, dates, times and places." "Slow your role son, you do realize that all of this happened over 40 years ago," said Deacon Myers. I said, "Yeah, I know but I wasn't there so I need some answers now. Come on with it!"

Deaconess Myers began to speak, again and said "Well, now that I think back, I vaguely remember that about the second year after Rev. Charles and the family arrived, the church had a secretary that was really crazy about Rev. Charles. The reason I remember that is because there *was* a confrontation between First Lady Lula and this secretary." I said, "Keep on talking Deaconess Susie." She said, "It's all slowly coming back to me now. You see, back then the church had two secretaries. One of them was Minnie Hardeman. Now Minnie was a good looking light skinned woman, but she was much older than Rev. Charles at that time. She might have liked Rev. Charles, but he was not interested in her. Minnie worked in the church office from Monday to Wednesday during the hours of 8:00 AM–4:00 PM.

The other secretary was a beautiful, young curvaceous lady by the name Mary Buford. Mary worked from Wednesday to Friday also during the hours of 8:00 AM–4:00 PM. So there was one day of the week when the two secretaries were in the office at the same time. Needless to say, there was always friction on Wednesdays because both of them wanted Rev. Charles. Like enmity between Jesus and Satan, Minnie and Mary butted heads as they competed for the Pastor's attention and affection. They each had their own desk and their office was right outside of the Pastor's Study. They each dressed provocatively and danced and pranced in front of Rev. Charles. For Mary it was no contest because Rev. Charles really liked Mary and he was at best very kind to Minnie." I asked Deaconess Myers, "So, what happened? Tell me about the confrontation."

She continued, "Well, this arrangement with the two secretaries continued for at least four years or so and as Rev. Charles got closer and closer to Mary Buford, Minnie Hardeman became more and more angry. So much so that she began to plot and scheme and leak information throughout the congregation about the nature of the cozy relationship between Rev. Charles and Mary Buford. Now, she would never flat out say that Rev. Charles was sleeping with Mary, but she painted a vivid enough picture so that people would draw their own conclusions. Remember, she wanted Rev. Charles too and she really didn't want to do or say anything that would lead back to her as the culprit or instigator. So she padded her words and covered her own tracks."

With a bit of an attitude I said, "Okay, Deaconess Myers, tell me about the confrontation!" She said, "Alright! I was just setting the stage and trying to remember all of the details as they occurred. The confrontation happened because of the tactics of Minnie Hardeman. Rev. Charles and Mary Buford did a lot of playing and flirting in the office and Mary made sure that it was more noticeable on Wednesdays. So Minnie came up with a sinister plan to dial Rev. Charles' house with the office telephone on speaker phone during one of Rev. Charles and Mary's playful, flirtatious moments. When this was done, of course First Lady Lula was on the other end of the telephone and she heard a very damaging sexually flirtatious exchange between her husband and one of his secretaries.

First Lady Lula dropped what she was doing and made a bee line down to the church, busted into the administrative office and saw Minnie sitting innocently at her desk. Minnie with a sheepish grin then pointed and directed Lula toward the closed door of the Pastor's Study. When First Lady Lula pushed opened the door and walked in, all hell broke loose. Mary Buford, the young buxom beauty was provocatively perched on Rev. Charles' desk with her arms around his neck and Rev. Charles was standing in between her legs with his arms around her waist and they were engaged in a very passionate kiss." I said to Deaconess Myers, "Say it aint so?" She answered, "It is so!"

Deaconess Myers continued, "Lula Mae grabbed Mary in the collar, backed her up against the wall and told her in plain English, 'If I ever catch you anywhere near my husband again, I'm going to beat you so bad, your own mother won't recognize you. I heard everything that the two of you were saying. Somehow one of you geniuses called my house with the phone on speaker and I heard everything. I heard you ask my husband to come on over here and lay hands on you. On top of that, I heard you

Joseph; tell her that you would do more than lay hands on her. I heard everything! Joseph, I will deal with you when we get home. As for you Mary Buford, your services as church secretary and Pastor's floozy are no longer needed and you are dismissed.' Mary Buford then sucked her teeth, snapped back and said, 'Who the hell are you? You didn't hire me and you sure enough can't fire me; tell her Joe–Joe!'"

"First lady Lula said, 'Joe–Joe, who in the hell is Joe–Joe and why is she calling you that? You better tell her *Joe–Joe* that she is fired or I'll take this to the Deacons and the Trustees and have them do it. As a matter of fact I'm going to do that anyway and suggest to them that her membership also be terminated as she is causing a great disturbance not only in the church but also in our marriage. So you might as well pack your bags little Ms. Thing, because the time of your departure is at hand.'" I asked Deaconess Myers as I was writing it all down, "So what happened next?" She said, "Rev. Charles then told Mary that he thought it would be best if she left and didn't come back. Mary rolled her eyes at Lula, winked at Rev. Charles and sexily sashayed out of the Pastor's Study, passed Minnie's desk, rolled her eyes at her also and under her breath called her a bitch. Mary then quietly disappeared and had not come back to the church."

I was still writing it all down as Deaconess Myers finished up and I said, "That was a lot of information. Do you have anything else?" Deacon Myers answered, "Well, there was more stuff but after that incident Rev. Charles was much more careful and after word got out about First Lady Lula hemming up Mary Buford, the overly flirtatious and brazen behavior of a lot of the women was curtailed. Those Jezebels learned to pick their moments which were mostly when First Lady Lula was nowhere around." I said to the Myers, "You all have been very helpful and I'm sure I have something to work with. I'm going to take what I have, process it, gather up the other information from First Lady Lula and the children and with all of it I know we'll get some answers. It's been a long day and I'm going to get ready to go, but before I do, cut me a piece of the coconut cake with the pineapple filling. Please? Thank You!"

The Search Intensifies!

IT IS GOOD THAT HE SHOULD SEARCH YOU OUT?
JOB 13:9

I was really intrigued by all of the information that I'd learned from the Myers concerning Rev. Charles and the church secretaries. Although it didn't tie directly into what we were searching for, I felt that it was significant enough to have on record. Again, I was actually taking notes like I was sitting in service and someone was preaching. The reason I was compelled to take notes was because they were talking so fast that I didn't want to miss anything. So in the best interest of the Charles family, I was forced to take a crash course in dictation so as not to leave out any vital or crucial details that might be helpful to the situation. I was eagerly anticipating sharing what I had been given with First Lady Lula, John, Matthew and Miriam. As I was going over my notes, piecing things together, and making complete sentences out of all the fragments, it came to me that at least one person, namely First Lady Lula, should have already known about this entire ordeal.

It was time for an update meeting between me and

the family. I called Miriam and told her to gather up the troops because I was coming over to find out what they had come up with and share with them what I had learned. She told me to give her a couple of days because she had to call John and Matthew to make sure they would be there. A couple of days went by and we all gathered once again at the Charles home; First Lady Lula, John, Matthew, Miriam and I. This time we all sat around the dining room table and got right down to business. I had my notes, John had his notes and Matthew had his notes. First Lady Lula had what appeared to be an old diary and Miriam had a few of the old Green Pastures Baptist Church anniversary journals.

First Lady Lula suggested that we have a word of prayer and as she began to pray we all joined hands and bowed our heads. She began praying and softly said, "All wise and everlasting Father, we humbly come before you asking that you would be with us as we search for understanding. Lord Jesus, guide our minds and guard our hearts. As we lean and depend on you for answers and closure, bless us and continue to ease our pain. For we know that all things work together for the good of them that love the Lord. In Jesus' name we pray, Amen." In response to that heart felt prayer, a collective 'Amen' was said by all.

John immediately took charge of the meeting. Still being motivated by anger at his deceased father, he wanted to share some of the things that he had found out, first. He angrily said, "I thought about what was suggested in terms of going back and talking to those old timers, those members who were around when daddy first came to Green Pastures, and I was led to perhaps the quietest person in the whole church. I had a conversation with the church sexton, Deacon Henry Spruill." Matthew jokingly asked, "Could you even understand what he was saying? Y–y–y–you kn–kn–kn–know h–h–h–how h–h–h–he talks." John had to laugh and then he answered, "Yes, it took a while but as I listened more closely I was able to decipher what he was saying. I had to handle Deacon Spruill very gingerly because I knew that he was a no–nonsense, country boy from the old school. I also knew that he was very loyal to daddy. He told me that he first met daddy 46 years ago when he first came up to New York from Macon, Georgia. He had no money, no job, and didn't know anybody in the city and when he asked daddy for directions to go to a job interview he said that daddy told him, 'I don't know where the place is that you are looking for but if you want a job, you can come and work for me as the church sexton.' And he has been there ever since."

John continued, "I asked Deacon Spruill if there was anything that he remembered that could possibly help the church find out what happened to the insurance money." Miriam asked, "John, why did you ask Deacon Spruill about the insurance money?" John answered, "If I had asked Deacon Spruill if he knew anything about whom daddy was messing with, he would have shut down on me and protected daddy's reputation. I had to use the subtle approach because of his loyalty toward *his* Pastor." Matthew sarcastically asked, "W–w–w–well wh–wh–wh–what d–d–did he say?" John responded, "He said, 'If you are really trying to ask me if I know who the young man is that says he's Rev. Charles' son, you are fishing with the wrong bait. I know nothing about that. I just do my job; serve the Lord and my Pastor. I'm not like those wicked women that used to work in the office for Rev.

Charles. Neither one of those women meant your father any good.'

I asked Deacon Spruill, 'What do you mean by that?' He said, 'I used to tell Rev. to be careful because those two women were vying for his affection and setting him up. I even told Rev. that one time while I was mopping the floor outside the office, I heard the phone ring like it was on a speaker. Then I heard First Lady Lula Mae answer the phone and all of sudden I heard Rev. Charles and that no good Mary Buford funning and saying stuff they ought not to have been saying. I peeked into the office and that old no good Minnie Hardeman sitting at her desk with an evil grin on her face. She didn't see me but I saw her and knew that she rang First Lady's phone on purpose. It was not long after that that your mother came storming into the office and I knew it was trouble. I told Rev. Charles that it was Minnie who called your mother. It was a set up, I tell you. Your father was a good man but those women were getting the best of him.'"

Matthew then asked John "Is that all that Deacon Spruill had to say?" John replied turning toward his mother, "Yes, that's all I got from him, but momma you never told us anything about this." First Lady Lula responded, I told you all that there would be some things that were swept under the rug that were going to come out. And a lot of these things, for my own sanity, I had to put out of my mind so that I could heal. Now, your father wasn't the best man, but he was good to us." Miriam replied nearly in tears, "Momma, why are you still trying to protect him? He's dead and gone and we are sitting here trying to undo his mess. We are here because he was cheating on you!"

I thought to myself, well, since we were already on the subject, this would be a good time for me to share what I had learned from the Myers. I interjected and told them, "I don't know what the connection is in finding out who the young man or his mother are but I have some similar information that I learned from speaking in depth to Deacon and Deaconess Myers. Everybody knows that Deacon and Deaconess Myers were serving at Green Pastures when Rev. Charles got here. Well, I don't know what this all means but they told me that there were a lot of women who were sweet on Rev. Charles. However, two women, Minnie Hardeman and Mary Buford and this one particular incident that Deacon Spruill told John, stood out in their minds above all the rest."

Miriam asked, "Well, what did they tell you?" I answered, "They basically told me the same thing that John just described. The only difference is that Deaconess Myers gave more detail. She told me that it was during the second year after Rev. Charles started, that the church had two secretaries. One was named Minnie Hardeman and the other was named Mary Buford. Minnie who was a light–skinned good looking older woman was infatuated with Rev. Charles but he was not interested in her. As Deaconess Myers put it, Rev. Charles knowing that she liked him, was at best very kind to her. Mary Buford, on the other hand, was a pretty young thing, with a vivacious body and she was absolutely crazy about Rev. Charles. And as quiet as it was kept, Rev. Charles was very fond of her as well."

Matthew asked, "Momma, can you remember any of this?" First Lady Lula answered, "To tell you the truth, I remember bits and pieces." John then said to me, "Come on and tell me more of what the Myers told you that was different from what Deacon Spruill told me." I continued, "Well, Deaconess Myers explained their work schedule and how Minnie worked from Monday to Wednesday and Mary worked from Wednesday to Friday. Of course Wednesday was showdown day, because they were both in the office at the same time and like Deacon Spruill said, they were both vying for Rev. Charles' affection and attention. Minnie being jealous of the attention that Rev. Charles was giving to Mary came up with the scheme to call First Lady Lula on speaker phone and have her listen in on Rev. Charles and Mary making sexual innuendoes toward each other. It worked like a charm and First Lady Lula; you quickly went down to the church and busted Rev. Charles and Mary Buford in a compromising position."

Miriam then angrily said, "Momma, I know you remember this, now tell us what happened." First Lady Lula answered, "Yes, I heard them flirting and talking dirty to each other on the phone. I didn't know that Minnie was the one who dialed the phone. I thought it was Joseph's carelessness. So I went down to the church. I remember going into that office and seeing your father standing between that woman's legs while she sat her behind on his desk and they were kissing and embracing. I snatched that heifer up so fast that she didn't know what hit her and then I fired her. Matthew said, "You fired her?" First Lady Lula responded, "Yes, I fired her and I told the Deacons and the Trustees that I wanted her removed from the church membership. As far as I know she moved out of state down to Alabama and we hadn't heard from her since that incident. Now, what does rehashing and reliving this story have to do with the answers that we are searching for? Mary Buford is long gone."

When First Lady Lula made that statement of finality, it signaled that it was time to adjourn the meeting.

We didn't even get to Matthews notes, First Lady Lula's diary or the church anniversary journals that Miriam had. As far as I was concerned it was time for me to go and we would continue at the next meeting.

THE SEARCH STALLS...

WHEN I HAD WAITED, FOR THEY SPAKE NOT, BUT STOOD
STILL, AND ANSWERED NO MORE...
JOB 32:16

We came away from the last meeting no closer to an answer then when we had first begun. With all of the information that had been gathered, with all of the ugly secrets of the past that had subsequently come out, we still don't know who made off with the money and prior to the money, who made off with the *honey*. It seemed as if everyone had gotten so caught up in the saga of the sexy secretary scandal that they had completely forgotten about the primary objective. The search had literally come to a stand still. Our primary objective *was* to try to gain some insight as to who the mystery man and his mother was and whether or not we could actually place them in Green Pastures or were they perhaps members of a sister church that we had fellowshipped with.

You do know that was a common practice for the good old boys club, the intermingling of Pastors with each others members. What? Don't act like you didn't know that there was a good old boys club among Pastors? Just like the police have a "Blue Wall of Silence," Pastors also have a good old boys club in which they do favors for each other, protect and cover for each other. These Pastors very often hooked each other up with the available and sometimes unavailable women within their congregations. While as their spiritual leaders, they should have been praying for these women, instead, they willingly offered them up as sacrificial lambs to ravenous wolves and allowed their constituents to *prey* on them. The crazy thing is that some of the woman felt obliged or were happy to be of assistance to their Pastors and happy to get what they were getting out of the deal. The truth is that the Pastors who rolled liked that (behaved in that manner) were big ballers (big spenders who live high maintenance lifestyles) and treated these women royally.

Most of these women, notice that I said most and not all, were single parents, who lived on fixed or limited incomes. To them, being picked up and chauffeured in a luxury car, and having a night out with a distinguished gentleman, role model in the community, prestigious and prominent Pastor at an exclusive restaurant, followed by a stay at a luxury hotel was an exciting change from their normal routine and daily grind. Gifts of cash and jewelry were also frequently given to show their appreciation and give incentive for the continuance of these encounters. In turn, the homes and apartments of these willing female participants became for the Pastors, respites and stopovers for meals, naps, and occasional sexual trysts. I am in no wise making excuses for these women based on their circumstances, because they all knew that most of these men were married. However, for some of them stepping out on their no good, no job having or minimum wage job having, anti–church, abusive husbands or boyfriends came quite easy.

As I began to think more and more about what was so vividly remembered concerning Rev. and Mrs. Charles and the incident with the secretary, I began to reason that there must be something else there. I am no private investigator but I did have a gut feeling about this. The recollection that Deacon and Deaconess Myers offered plus the recapitulation of events Deacon Spruill shared with John, along with First Lady Lula's almost forced input, leads me to believe that there is more to this than meets the eye. Yes, there were a number of other events, indiscretions and run–ins throughout Rev. Charles' pastorate, some more memorable than others; but for one to be so strongly etched in the minds and memories of so many, certainly deserves a closer look. However, I needed to do a little more digging. We had merely scratched the surface and in order to get the answers we were seeking we needed to get beneath the surface.

If Deacon and Deaconess Myers, Deacon Spruill and First Lady Lula had remembered this particular incident, I was certain that if I kept on searching in regards to the same, someone else would have some relevant information. In keeping in line with what I had originally surmised I again wanted to tap into the old timers and long time members of Green Pastures Baptist Church. I needed to further communicate with those who were trustworthy and would give an unbiased account with a reasonable amount of veracity. I needed to talk with those who at this point had nothing to lose and nothing to gain. As it was, I had a pretty good relationship with just about everybody in the church. I was quite friendly, well liked and most people naturally opened up to me because I was so close to the Charles family. They also gravitated toward me because I was the Minister of Music and every one felt a special closeness with me; some more than others, if you know what I mean.

I really needed to narrow down the potential data base and zero directly in on those who could possibly be of some significant assistance. I needed to shift my thinking, change my thought process, modify my mode of operation and come up with a new plan based on the information I had already been given. I decided that rather than pursue answers to the original questions of who this mystery mother and son were, I needed to push the envelope concerning the events that everyone else seemed to remember in their own way. I felt like if I had stuck with the First Lady Lula and Mary Buford drama, then that particular drama would lead me to the baby mama drama.

Why was the same story being told by so many different people? It kind of reminded of the Gospels; you know, Matthew, Mark, Luke and John. They each had a target group and purpose for their accounts of Jesus' life and ministry. I don't have time to get into a long Bible lesson but I will share this much. The Gospels according to Matthew was written for the Jews, Mark was written for the Romans or the Christians in Rome, Luke was written for the Greeks and Gentiles and John was written for the new Christians and searching non–Christians. When I compare this scenario of the Gospel *writers* and how they each had a different view of the story of Jesus, to the three accounts of the story of Rev. Charles and his secretary, perhaps securing a fourth version would bring some much needed clarity and revelation. No, I am not saying that the actual life and ministry of Rev. Charles parallels that of Jesus. Jesus was in all points tempted just as we are and yet He was without sin. Rev. Charles on the other hand, was likewise tempted, fell to the temptations and great was the fall of him.

My feeling was that Deacon and Deaconess Myers, Deacon Spruill and First Lady Lula Mae were not the only ones that remembered what happened between Rev. Charles and his secretary Mary Buford. I am of the opinion that there were some other women within the congregation who also wanted Rev. Charles, yet they did not have the access to him like Mary Buford. In fact, because of the purposefully damaging information that Minnie Hardeman was leaking out, a lot of these women also knew what went down and they were jealous of and hating on Mary Buford. Basically, because they couldn't get to Rev. Charles like Mary Buford did, they all joined the bandwagon in spreading the news of what they heard had transpired, in addition to adding their own two cents.

I was actually torn because on the one hand I wanted to help First Lady Lula and the family to bring closure in these matters and on the other hand I still felt a certain sense of loyalty to Rev. Charles. I know at this point that everyone was already dogging Rev. Charles out, but I didn't want my involvement to add to the barrage of character assassinations being leveled against the memory of Rev. Charles. I tried to pray but I couldn't even do that because I wasn't sure that God was pleased with me being involved in digging up old dirt on Rev. Charles. I know God understood my willingness to help the family and the church, but I was struggling with whether or not God would punish me for bringing to light the past sins of my Pastor. Rev. Charles was good to me and I, believe it or not, even wrestled with the thought of the ghost of Rev.

Joseph M. Charles, III coming back to haunt me because of my participation.

So, even though the search was somewhat temporarily stalled and we hit some unforeseen road blocks, all hope was not lost. We were delayed but we would not be denied. Perhaps, God, in the midst of it all was yet teaching a valuable life lesson on patience and timing. God's timing is not our timing and while we are waiting for answers there is a manner in which we must wait. The Bible says in Psalm 27:14… *Wait on the Lord: be of good courage, and He shall strengthen thine heart: wait, I say, on the Lord.*

The Search Resumes...

LET US SEARCH AND TRY OUR WAYS, AND TURN
AGAIN TO THE LORD.
LAMENTATIONS 3:40

Well, I'm glad I don't have to go *all* the way back to the
drawing board, but this paradigm shift is going to make
things a great deal more interesting. I was wondering
where I should go and to whom should I turn to in this
next phase of interrogation? I had some questions and
I needed some answers. I was led to go right back to
Deaconess Myers. I went to the Myers home once again
but this time I met with Deaconess Myers only. I asked,
"Do you know of anyone who was close to Mary Buford
when she was here at Green Pastures? I figured that Mary
Buford had to have had a friend or two at the church."
Deaconess Myers answered, "First of all she was not
well liked and received among most of the women in the
church because the news was out that she was the home–
wrecking hussy that was messing with Rev. Charles." I
said, "But there had to be somebody that she was close to.

She must have had a girlfriend or two that she hung out with and shared her experiences with."

Deaconess Myers said, "I really need to think long and think hard about this one." In fact, she said, "Let me look back in one of these old church anniversary journals because if I remember correctly I believe that there were some personal ads or business ads placed in one of them by Mary Buford and her business partner *Ms.* Claretha Davison." I asked, "Who in the world is Claretha Davison? I know a Claretha Slade, she sings on the Gospel Chorus, but I don't know a Claretha Davison." Deaconess Myers responded, "Claretha Slade and Claretha Davison are one and the same. Davison was her maiden name and then she married Deacon Archie Slade just two years after his wife Deaconess Mabel Slade died. I personally think she was messing with Deacon Slade all along, even before his poor wife died, but that's just me. I don't know why he married that young girl anyhow. She was half his age." I said, "That's why he married her. Hello?"

Deaconess Myers continued, "Mary Buford and Claretha Davison owned and operated a women's clothing boutique where they sold some of the provocative clothing that they wore. Not only did they have their own store but they were their best customers and put on a fashion show *every* Sunday." As it turned out, Deaconess Myers found the full page color ad in one of the church anniversary journals early in Rev. Charles' tenure that featured a beautiful colored picture of Mary and Claretha standing in front of their boutique. It was *some* ad for that day and time. They were both scantily clad in red, with skirts above the knees, low plunging neck lines accenting their heavy cleavage, fishnet stockings, high heeled shoes and each of them with a one of a kind original hat on their heads. They were standing in a sexy pose pointing to the sign on their store that read, "Virtuosity!" and under that, Exquisite and Elegant Women's Wear.

I asked Deaconess Myers, "Were Mary and Claretha really that close?" She said, "They were so close that every time you saw one of them you saw the other. And if you didn't see them together it was because one of them was up in somebody's husband's face and the other one was standing guard." Then I asked, "Whatever happened to Mary and Claretha's friendship?" Deaconess Myers answered, "Well, after that incident with Rev. Charles, First Lady Lula Mae and Mary, their friendship kind of fell apart."

I asked, "Why would that incident cause their friendship to fall apart?" Deaconess Myers responded, "Well, because, after that incident, Mary Buford left town. And when she left town, she left Claretha holding the proverbial bag concerning their boutique. Claretha was good at what she did, but Mary was the heart and soul of the business, and her charm and charisma kept the customers coming. In Claretha's mind, Mary was planning to leave all along. She felt the incident wasn't enough to make Mary leave town. She understood that it was essential for Mary to leave the church, but she felt that Mary had already made plans to relocate but used the incident as her excuse to walk out on her and the business."

I said, "Whoa! That's deep. What ever happened to the business?" Deaconess Myers said, "Well as far as I know, Claretha barely kept the store going for about a year and then she sold it for a nice profit but had to give Mary Buford half of the profit because they were co–owners." I asked, "I thought you said their friendship fell apart?" Deaconess Myers answered, "They weren't good friends at the time but they had to settle their business matters. After Mary left the church, Claretha was still attending and putting on her fashion show every week. It was about six or seven years after that when Deaconess Mabel Slade died and Claretha publicly took up with her husband. You *need* to go and talk with *Mrs.* Claretha Slade. Notice that I said Mrs. Slade and not Deaconess Slade. She might have taken Mabel's husband, but she will never, I mean never be a Deaconess." I told Deaconess Myers, "I've got to get ready to go now, but I want to thank you so much for all you have shared with me. You once again have been very helpful. God bless you and goodnight."

When I left Deaconess Myers' home, I immediately began thinking about my next course of action. I needed to talk with the former Ms. Claretha Davison, now known as Mrs. Claretha Slade. This should be easy because Claretha was a member of the Gospel Chorus. As a matter of fact we had a regularly scheduled choir rehearsal coming up on Saturday morning at 10:00 AM and Claretha, now much older and classier in her style of dress, never missed a choir rehearsal. We had a pretty good rehearsal and as I was about to close out, I made an announcement. I leaned into the microphone and said, "I would like to meet with Sister Claretha Slade for about ten or fifteen minutes right after choir rehearsal." Claretha said jokingly, "What do you want to meet with me for? I didn't do anything." I answered, "I know you didn't do anything. I just need to talk to you."

As soon as choir rehearsal was dismissed, I led Claretha to my office. Yes, I was a privileged Minister of Music because not only did I have keys to the church, but I also had my own office. It wasn't that much bigger than a nice walk–in closet, but it was *my* office. I told

Claretha, "Please have a seat." She said, "What is this all about?" I answered, "I know you know about everything that's going on with the illegitimate mystery son of Rev. Charles, the inheritance money and all of that, but I want to talk to you about something else. I have been trying to help First Lady Lula and the family bring some closure to this whole episode, but there are a few missing pieces."

Claretha said, "Well, where do I fit in and how can I help you?" I responded, "I don't know what the connection is yet but I do know about the incident many years ago with Rev. Charles, First Lady Lula and Mary Buford. And I recently found out that you and Mary were not only good friends but also business partners." Claretha said, "Yes, that' right. We *were* friends and we *were* business partners, but she walked out on me. Yes, she did her little dirt and had her thing with Rev. Charles, but that was no reason for her to desert me, walk out and leave me. We were close friends. She told me she loved Rev. Charles and that she wasn't going anywhere until he left his wife, but as soon as that incident happened, she went running off to Alabama."

I asked her, "How do you know that she went to Alabama?" Claretha answered, "I know she moved to Alabama because that's where her high school sweetheart, and the real love of her life was in prison. As matter of fact, he was fixing to get out right around the time she left. She told me that herself." Then I asked Claretha, "Was Mary Buford from Alabama?" Claretha answered, "Yes, Mary was from Wilsonville, Alabama and that jailbird Calvin was from Thomasville, Alabama. That's where Mary ran off to when she left. She went to Thomasville and hooked back up with Calvin. I guess she never really got him out of her system. I know they used to communicate by phone and by letter when he was locked up. And I know she used to put money on the books for him, but she told me she was cutting him off and that she would never move back down south to be with him."

I said, "It must have been a real shock to you when she went back to Alabama." Claretha said, "I really didn't know where she went at first, but when I finally sold our store and settled that business she called me and told me to send her check to a Thomasville, Alabama address. That's when I realized that she had hooked back up with Calvin. We called each other occasionally but it was not like it once was." Then I said, "So let me ask you this, Claretha. Where is Mary Buford now?" Claretha answered, "With all due respect, I really don't care where Mary Buford is now. But if you must know, Mary *is* back in Brooklyn, New York. She has been back in Brooklyn for over thirty something years. She has been a member of the Mt. Moriah Baptist Church for just as long, where the Rev. P. J. Dixon is the Pastor and Mary is president of the Pastor's Aide. Didn't you see her at the musical that was held for Rev. Charles the night before his funeral?"

I asked Claretha, "You mean to tell me that Mary was at Rev. Charles' funeral." Claretha said, "No, I didn't see her at the funeral, but she was at the wake and the musical. She was definitely there and she was trying to be as inconspicuous as possible but that all went out of the window when she had to go up to the podium and get her nephew, Mark, who had broken down while he was giving tribute to Rev. Charles." I said, "I specifically remember that because it stood out in my mind as strange." Then I asked in surprise, "You mean to tell me that Mark Houston is Mary Buford's nephew?" Claretha answered, "Yes, when Mary Buford left and went down to Alabama, she married Calvin and Calvin's last name is Houston. When she came back to New York, she came back as Mary Houston. Not only that but she brought her sister–in–law's child with her. The reason Mary left Calvin is because he ended up back in jail and Mary said that Calvin's sister was strung out on drugs, so she took custody of her sister–in–law's son, Mark and raised him all by herself."

I said to Claretha, "I know I have kept you for too long now, but why then is Mark Houston a member of Green Pastures and Mary over at Mt. Moriah?" Claretha responded, "Yes, you have kept me for too long and I probably have said too much, but if it is going to be of some help, let me leave you with this. Mary couldn't come back to Green Pastures, but she always told me that she was quite fond of youth educational programs at Green Pastures. From the day care all the way up through the 12th grade academy, as well as all of the various youth ministries and she wanted Mark to grow up in those programs. So she made sure that Mark, her nephew, experienced that best that Green Pastures had to offer in that regard."

I said, "I understand that but Mark is a grown man and he is still an active member of Green pastures." Claretha responded, "Well, as Mark grew up and became a man, he was already steeped in the activities of Green Pastures and Green Pastures is where he remained. All of his friends were here. From day care on through high school, this young man being raised by his aunt through marriage but he had a huge extended family at Green Pastures. And because Mary couldn't come back to Green Pastures, she found her niche over at Mt. Moriah. You see, after she couldn't have Rev. Charles and her husband went back to jail for a long time, she became the mistress of Rev. P. J. Dixon, and was hoping to become the first lady of Mt. Moriah."

I then said to Claretha, "Wow! You have blown my mind with the information that you have given me. Please forgive me for writing while you were talking but there was so much that I didn't want to miss anything. This definitely is the missing piece to the puzzle. You better go on and get out of here before Deacon Slade comes looking for you. I don't want him to be mad with me for keeping you so long. You know I will fight an old crusty deacon."

THE SEARCH CULMINATES

AND I GAVE MY HEART TO SEEK AND SEARCH OUT BY WISDOM
CONCERNING ALL THINGS THAT ARE DONE UNDER HEAVEN...
ECCLESIASTES 1:13

This entire process has been grueling, arduous and not to mention overwhelming. However, I finally, *finally* feel like I am getting somewhere and making considerable progress. In my heart of hearts I really wanted some answers to bring closure not just for me, but more so for First Lady Lula, the family and the congregation. They asked me for my help and because I loved Rev. Charles and I love them as well, I was honored to help them and I consented to doing it with my whole heart. With everything coming more into focus, I now had to take some time for myself to sit down and put all of the pieces together. Everything that I had learned up to this point, even the things that others might have thought were insignificant, I chronicled and catalogued. I didn't want to leave any stone unturned.

In the past six to seven months since Rev. Charles died and this whole story broke, I had done so much note-taking, scribbling and writing, searching and digging, gone to meeting after meeting, compiled lists and narrowed them down by the process of elimination, made numerous phone calls and talked to so many scores of people that I was literally walking around like a zombie. However, this last bit of information that I received from Claretha Slade has given me a burst of energy and a great deal of hope. I didn't know right away what it all meant, but I knew there was a glimmer of sanity and a flicker of clarity somehow intertwined within this sordid entanglement of iniquity and intrigue.

I cleared off my dining room table, which was quite a task because it was covered with sheet music and newspapers. Then I turned off my cell phone and my home phone. I literally shut myself in from the outside world and with blinders on, got down to the business at hand. The same table that I had just cleared was quickly filled with everything that I'd gathered pertaining to the Rev. Charles epoch. In order to piece things together, I used this time for myself to go over everything that I knew and everything that I didn't know from the very beginning.

This is what I know. I know that 46 years ago Rev. Joseph M. Charles, III was called to Pastor the Green Pastures Baptist Church. Upon his acceptance of the call, part of his benefit package included two $500,000.00 insurance policies which of course totaled $1,000,000.00. Now, providing he remained on as Pastor for a minimum of 25 years, the church was to be the beneficiary of one of the policies and his family was to be the beneficiaries of the other as specified by him. He served more than 25 years and both policies were paid in full.

I also know that when Rev. Charles came on as Pastor, he and his wife Lula Mae had one son, John. About five years after that they had another son named Matthew. Maybe another five years or so after that their daughter Miriam was born and she indeed was daddy's little girl. I know that Rev. Charles loved his wife and especially loved his children. I know that Rev. Charles, in addition to being a family man was a learned spiritual leader with an earned doctorate, a charismatic figure who exuded confidence, and the ideal picture perfect man in the eyes of many women. I also know that the women did not hesitate in coming after him, even knowing his marital status.

I know that in the midst of it all, Rev. Charles had some outside interest that resulted in several affairs over the years. I know of one extramarital affair in particular that captured the attention of the entire Green Pastures Baptist Church. I know that it commenced approximately two years after Rev. Charles started as Pastor and lasted for another three or four years. I know that it involved Rev. Charles and one of the secretaries of Green Pastures by the name of Mary Buford. I know that their affair resulted in a confrontation between First Lady Lula Mae and Mary Buford, with Mary Buford getting the worst end of it. I also know that as a result of the confrontation Mary Buford was fired from her position as church secretary and her membership at Green Pastures was terminated.

I know that after Mary Buford was run out of the church, she relocated to Thomasville, Alabama. Coincidentally she relocated at around the same time her childhood sweetheart, Calvin Houston, was being released from prison. Upon his release, they married and Mary Buford became Mary Houston. I also know that shortly after their marriage, Calvin reverted to a life of crime and went back to jail for a considerably longer sentence and

Mary decided not to wait for him. She left him, divorced him and a few years later she moved back to Brooklyn, New York.

I know that when Mary Houston came back to Brooklyn she came back with a little boy named Mark Houston, who was supposedly the son of Calvin's sister. That part I'm not so sure about because even when I got this information from Claretha, Calvin's sister was never given a name. Claretha said that Mary never told her Calvin's sister's name. Calvin's sister supposedly lived with Calvin and Mary while they were in Alabama and she was strung out on drugs and not able to properly care for little Mark. So, Mary got legal custody of him and brought him up to New York for a better life.

I also know that upon her return, she became a member of the Mt. Moriah Baptist Church and carried on a longtime affair with Rev. P. J. Dixon, who was the Pastor. That affair resulted in Rev. Dixon and his wife getting a divorce, which thrilled Mary because she was *almost* a first lady. I know that from the time Mary brought Mark Houston up from Alabama, she enrolled him in the day care program and the academy at Green Pastures for the entirety of his school aged years. I also know that Mark also attended and was an active member of Green Pastures Baptist Church from the time he set foot in New York even up to the present time.

I know and recall that this same Mark Houston, who sings with the Male Chorus under my tutelage, had a memorable meltdown at Rev. Charles' wake and musical tribute. I also know and distinctly remember the last thing the Mark Houston said before he was rescued by a strange, veiled woman that turned out to be the infamous Mary Buford a.k.a. Mary Houston. The last thing that

Mark Houston said was that, 'if I had a father, I would have wanted my father to be just like Rev. Charles.' I also felt and discerned that there was some underlying substantiation to that statement.

I know that after Rev. Charles died and his family received their $500,000.00 inheritance, there was a major problem when the church went to collect their $500,000.00 inheritance. I know that the church was informed by the insurance company that they couldn't collect on the policy because the check had already been issued to a young man who said he was Rev. Charles' son. I also know that about ten years ago Rev. Charles redirected the potential proceeds from the policy that were supposed to be for the church to an unknown, unnamed male beneficiary who at the time of collection, was in his mid-thirties.

Now, I am no rocket scientist, neither am I Rhodes scholar, but in this case I don't think a rocket scientist or road scholar is necessary. It's not hard to figure out that Mark Houston is the illegitimate son of Rev. Charles and Mary Buford-Houston. Maybe it's a stretch and I'm reaching just a bit. Maybe I'm over exaggerating and trying to force the pieces of a twisted puzzle to fit together. Maybe this is merely speculatory on my part. Although I have a strong feeling about this I have not shared this theory with anyone as of yet. As far as I was concerned the search was over and I had found the 'golden child.' My next course of action would prove to be the definitive and deciding factors in this entire quagmire. I needed to go straight to the horse's mouth and talk directly to Mary Buford-Houston and Mark Houston. How was I going to pull this off?

The Confirmation...

BEHOLD, WHILE THOU YET TALKEST THERE WITH THE KING, I
ALSO WILL COME IN AFTER THEE, AND CONFIRM THY WORDS.

I KINGS 1:14

I had already made up my mind that the next time I called First Lady Lula and the family together for a meeting, it would be to reveal to them all of the answers they were looking for. I didn't want any preliminary meetings, or any partial answers. I didn't want any more speculations or insinuations. I wanted to deliver the goods, present the facts, and close the chapter. I really wanted to just get this over with so that *everyone,* including me could move on with their lives.

As I was reviewing my theory and preparing myself to make actual contact with Mark Houston and Mary Buford–Houston, something else came to me. It dawned on me that I had never even once considered talking with the person who preceded me as Minister of Music. When I came on board almost twenty years ago, the church had a retirement banquet for Brother Albert Best, who was the Minister of Music for over forty years. That means that he was there fourteen years before Rev. Charles became Pastor.

Not only was Best, which is what everybody called him, already there when Rev. Charles got there, they also had a great friendship and brotherly relationship. Best was one of those cool, jerry–curl wearing, smooth cats who never left the 1970's. In fact, I learned how to serve my Pastor and be faithful over my gift by watching and emulating Best before I started at Green Pastures. So my relationship with Rev. Charles was a natural transition because I endeavored to be to him what Best was to him. Albert Best was Rev. Charles' friend, homeboy, lookout, go–between, listening ear, chauffeur, supplier, and personal Minister of Music. Whenever Rev. Charles preached out and did out of town revivals Albert Best was there. So I knew that Best had some old war stories, but in all of the confusion I had completely forgotten about him and excluded him from the equation.

When Best retired from Green Pastures, he moved back down to his hometown of Wilmington, North Carolina. He was even playing for another church down there to keep himself busy, but of course it is a much slower pace. I believe he was playing for the St. Phillips A.M.E. church in Wilmington. Well, I gave Albert Best a call. When I called him, he was excited to hear from me. The phone rang and the voice on the other end said, "Hello, you've reach the Best." I said, "Albert Best is the best." He said right away, "I *know* who this is. This is my main man. Doc, when I grow up I want to be just like you. You are the baddest cat out there. Nobody can handle a Hammond B3 organ like you can." He always said that to me every time he saw me or every time we talked. And I always responded, "Man, I just trying to keep up with you." He then asked, "What's going on up there in Brooklyn?" I said, "It's the same old, same old."

Then He said, "I heard about all the mess that's going on up there in Green Pastures." I said, "Yeah, it's been a rough ride, but that's exactly what I called you about." He said, "What do you need, man? What do you want to know?" When he opened up that door I stepped right in and said, "I've been helping First Lady Lula, John, Matthew and Miriam try to find out exactly who this unknown son is that made off with the money. Not only that, but we've also been trying to figure out who his mother is and whether or not they were ever a part of Green Pastures. Best, do you know anything about that? Can you shine a little light on the situation? Come on, help a brother out."

He said, "Do I know anything about it? Man, I was there when it all started. I was there when it all went down. I was right smack dab in the middle of it all. It wasn't no fun if I wasn't getting none. Yes, I know who the son is. The son is Mark Houston and Mark Houston has been a part of Green Pastures Baptist Church ever since his mother Mary Buford brought him up to New York from Alabama when he was a little boy. He was raised up right along with his half brothers and sister and he knew that Rev. Charles was his father. Rev. Charles swore me to secrecy and I have never told a living soul until now, until this very moment. You dig?" I said, "Well, come on doc, the cat is out of the bag now. How did this all begin?"

Best then said, "I hope you have a few minutes and I'll give you the low down on the show down. When Rev. Charles first started messing with Mary Buford it was because we went out on a double date. Rev. was with Mary and I was with that fine, tall drink of water, Ms. Claretha

Davison. What Claretha and I had was hot a heavy but it was short lived. On the flip side, Rev. Charles really took a liking to Mary and then Mary put it on him, he was wide open. I tried to warn him. I told him to be careful because Mary had long term plans for him, but he wouldn't listen to me." I said, "So what happened?" Best continued, "Well, after First Lady Lula and Mary had that run in and Mary left town, she ended up in Alabama. Needless to say, we made quite a few visits to Alabama, Thomasville to be exact. Mary married her childhood sweetheart, some dude named Calvin. Rev. Charles was hurt and upset when Mary married Calvin, so he kept accepting invitations to preach revivals down in Thomasville, Alabama and as soon as we arrived, he would send for Mary. That's when Mary got pregnant. I told Rev. Charles that woman was trouble."

I said, "So, how did she end up back in New York?" Best said, "From the time that heifer found out she was pregnant, which by then she had already left Calvin, she had made up her mind that she was going to have the baby and that she was coming back to New York. Rev. Charles desperately tried to talk her out of it, but she didn't want to hear it. She promised not to make any trouble for him, but she did let him know from jump–street that their son would be in his life. Honestly, I don't know how she talked Rev. Charles into allowing Mark not only to come up to New York, but the crazy plan of him being raised up side by side with his wife and kids right in Green Pastures Baptist Church. I told him that it was a crazy idea but she must have put it on him again. He said that she was going to handle everything and she would condition Mark to make everyone think that she was his aunt and to never let anyone know that Rev. was his father. I didn't think it could be done, but they made a liar out of me."

I asked him, "So, nobody else knew?" He said, "As far as I know, I was the only one and I swore to my buddy that I would never tell. Mary even kept it from her one time closest friend Claretha." I said, "Best, let me ask you just one more question before I let you go." He said, "Sure man, what is it?" I said, "How did you feel carrying this secret around for well over thirty years?" He answered, "To tell you the truth man, it was a living hell. I tried to ignore it. I had nightmares about the whole situation blowing up in Rev. Charles' face, while he was still alive. I even tried to reach out and do some father and son things with Mark. I took him to ball games. I helped him through puberty and through his awkward teenage years. I gave him advice about sex and women. Man, I hated it. I hated it because I loved Lula Mae and those kids and I knew it wasn't fair to them. But I also knew it was twice as unfair for Mark and I loved that kid. This boy knew this man was his daddy and his mother had twisted his mind and convinced him not to say or do anything that would remotely draw attention to the facts, and he did just that. He lived with it all of his life. Do you know what kind of mental trauma that boy had to live with. I was surprised that he didn't turn out to be a drug addict, alcoholic or serial killer. I thought he would end up in jail or be suicidal, but he dealt with it. He even knew that I knew and yet he still would never talk about it or even bring it up because his mother had him so messed up."

I said, "Man, that's real heavy. You are some kind of friend. God bless you." Then Best said, "Man, you are some kind of friend too and I don't envy you because I know that you have the task of telling Lula Mae, John,

Matthew and Miriam what I have just told you. I will be praying for you and if you need me, just call and I'll come running. The other thing is that when the rest of the church finds out, all hell is going to break loose. Everyone is going to be mad as hell that Rev. Charles played them like fools and allowed his children to be raised side by side with his bastard son, right up under, not only his wife's nose, but everyone that he preached to, everyone that he taught, and everyone that he chastised, rebuked and corrected." I said, "Yes, I know what's coming, but I really just want closure for the family. So, listen, man. I want to thank you for all of your help and for your candor and honesty and I'll talk to you real soon. In fact, I will call you and let you know how everything went. I love you, man. You are the Best." Then Best said, "No, you are *the man!* I'll holler at you later."

It's A Set Up

...AND I WILL BUILD AGAIN THE RUINS THEREOF, AND I
WILL SET IT UP.
ACTS 15:16

Wow! After talking with Brother Best and receiving definitive confirmation of my theorem and after my carefully thought out hypothesis was proven, I had to change my mind about going straight to the horse's mouth. Initially, I was going to set up a meeting with Mark Houston and Mary Buford, tell them what information I had gathered and then flat out ask them where they fit in the whole scheme of things. I had made up my mind to throw all caution to the wind and ask Mary Buford, first of all, if she was indeed Mark Houston's mother and not his aunt as she had everyone to believe. I had intended to ask Mark if he was indeed Rev. Charles' illegitimate son and if he was the one who made off with the money that was supposed to be designated for the church. I had psyched myself up and although I was in a precarious position and the subject matter was extremely touchy, I was ready to confront them not only on behalf of the Charles family but also on behalf of the members of the Green Pastures Baptist Church.

In addition to my prospective meeting with Mark Houston and Mary Buford, I'd also prepared myself to meet with First Lady Lula, John, Matthew and Miriam, to bring them up to speed on the progress that I had made and finally give them the shocking information that they've so desperately been waiting for. Deacon Myers and Brother Jones were also eagerly waiting to hear from me. Because of their positions, they were becoming the sounding boards and victims of undue pressure from the membership of Green Pastures. To be honest, I really was not looking forward to any of the three meetings, but I knew that they each had to be done. Well, with all that I had intended to do, my conversation with Brother Robert Best has caused a change in plans, a shift in sequences and a modification in momentum. What would have been three separate and distinct meetings; I have since decided should now and must be one collective meeting, with all of the involved parties.

How I was going to get everyone together and how I was going to conduct the meeting was the next big challenge for me. The delicate and sensitive nature of the entire ordeal coupled together with the dangerously inflammatory probability would certainly make for an interesting and tension filled meeting. After all, it had been nearly nine months since Rev. Charles died and nearly nine months since everyone was informed that the church's insurance money was left to Rev. Charles' love child. For nearly nine months everyone had been trying to find out who this love child was. Isn't it ironic that the normal gestation period for a developing baby is nine months, and it works out to be the same amount of time this discovery of a thirty–something year old man had been festering? For nearly nine months, the hearts and the minds of the entire Green Pastures Baptist Church, First Lady Lula, John, Matthew and Miriam have been impregnated with the thought of the recent *birth* announcement of a grown man. Everyone paced the proverbial floor with the intensity of an expectant father, but when this child would be delivered, they would not be handing out cigars.

I needed to secure a date, time and place for this historic meeting. I came up with Saturday, October 21, 2002 at 1:00 PM in the conference room of Green Pastures. I called First Lady Lula Mae and when she answered the telephone I got straight to the point. I said, "First Lady, I am calling you and the family together for a meeting with Deacon Myers, Brother Jones and hopefully the ones whom we have been seeking." She said, "You mean you found out who these people are? I told her, "I'm not going to discuss any of that now. However, all things will be disclosed at the meeting, which will be held on Saturday, October 21 at 1:00 PM in the conference room." She said, "Alright sweetie, you sound like you really mean business. I will inform John, Matthew and Miriam and we will see you there." I answered, "Thank you so much, First Lady and I'll see yawl there."

I then called Deacon Myers and we did a three–way call with Brother Jones. I informed the both of them that significant progress had been made and it was time for a meeting with First Lady Lula, the children and the mystery mother and child in question. Deacon Myers asked, "I take it you have found the mother and child?" I answered, "Yes, and it will all be revealed at the meeting." Brother Jones asked, "O, you are just going to let us sweat it out?" I said, "Yes, you all are going to have to wait until the meeting just like everybody else." Brother Jones responded, "Well, I don't mind waiting, just as long as we get to the bottom of this whole thing. By the way, where is the meeting and what time should we be there?" I answered, "The meeting is going to take place in the conference room of the church on Saturday, October 21 at 1:00 PM." Deacon Myers asked, "Should we ask the church's attorney to be present?" I said, "No, I don't think it is necessary at this point. Perhaps in the subsequent meetings to follow, we will need legal council and then request the attorney's presence." Then Deacon Jones and Brother Jones both stated that they would no doubt, be in attendance. And I ended the three way call by saying to them, "You two guys have a blessed evening and I will see you at the meeting." They each said, "Thank you and good night."

My next course of action would prove to be the most challenging. It was time for me to call Mark Houston. It wasn't totally unthinkable for me to call or communicate with him; after all he was a member of one of the choirs under my charge. He sang with the Male Chorus of Green Pastures and was a faithful member in good standing. I thought that maybe Mark might have considered it a little strange for me to call him for something not relating to the choir, but I had to do it. I called and the phone rang twice and then a voice on the other end said, "Hello, Mark speaking." I said, "Hey there, Brother Mark, this is your favorite Minister of Music." He said, "Yes, you indeed are my favorite. How are you doing and to what do I owe the pleasure of your call?" I said, "I'm doing fine and the reason I've called is because there has been some recent issues as of late concerning the church, the passing of Rev. Charles and possibly including you that has prompted a meeting. Your presence along with your aunt, Mary has been requested at this meeting."

Mark responded, "A meeting? I knew it was coming and I *do* know what it's all about. In fact, I have been waiting my whole life for this meeting to finally come. When and where is the meeting supposed to take place?" I said, "Well, it is set for this coming Saturday, October 21 at 1:00 PM in the conference room of the church." Mark then asked, "Who else is going to be at this meeting?" I said, "Mark, I'm going to be completely honest with you. I know this is not an easy time for you but you need to know that First Lady Lula, John, Matthew, Miriam, and Deacon Myers the chairman of the Deacons, Brother Jones the chairman of the Trustees and me, will be there." Mark said, "I don't have a problem with that. I actually expected all of the aforementioned parties to be involved in this one way or another." Then I asked Mark, "Are you going to be there?" He answered, "By the grace of God and with the Lord as my strength I will be there."

I said, "Well, is it possible that you can contact your aunt Mary and see if she will agree to come to the meeting?" Mark said, "I don't see it being a problem at all. I will contact her and I am one hundred percent sure that she will be there with bells on." I then said to Mark, "So, what you are telling me is *I* don't have to call Mary Buford and you will pass along all of the information concerning the meeting?" Mark said, "I told you I would take care of it and I can guarantee you that Mary Buford–Houston will be there." Needless to say, I was satisfied with what Mark had said concerning Mary, because she didn't really know me and although I was prepared to call and speak with her, Mark's guarantee of her attendance suited me fine. The bottom line for me was that finally all parties involved would be contacted and present at the meeting and all of the unanswered questions would be addressed. It's been a long time coming but I know a change is going to come.

THE LONG AWAITED MEETING

LET US MEET TOGETHER IN THE HOUSE OF GOD, WITHIN THE
TEMPLE, AND LET US SHUT THE DOORS OF THE TEMPLE...
NEHEMIAH 6:10

This is the day that the Lord has made and I will rejoice and be glad in it. I know it almost sounds like a cliché but in this particular instance, it is not. Not only is this the day the Lord has made, it is also the day when it will all go down. Today is the day. To tell you the truth, it felt like this day, Saturday, October 21, 2002, would never come. Oh, but it is finally here and though I am rejoicing, there is still a tinge of sadness. There is a bittersweet oxymoronic undertone and there is also a satirically ironic overtone. On the one hand I am rejoicing because closure would finally come for First Lady Lula and the family and on the other hand I am somewhat disheartened because when all of the previously hidden information comes out, so many will be hurt by the truth, the secrets and the lies. Nevertheless, the time has come and now is when secrets of all hearts shall be disclosed.

I had arrived at the church early in an effort to make sure that everything was set up properly. The church's conference room was a very large room with a very large conference table that seated twelve. However, I figured that it would be safe to strategically arrange the seating just in case this volatile situation got out of hand. Short of actually placing nametags on the table, I felt that the seating arrangements needed to be carefully thought out and monitored. Knowing what would potentially come out at this meeting, and knowing the level of stress and emotionalism this entire saga has generated, it was better to be safe than sorry. As I was in the process of moving the chairs around, I was joined by Deacon Myers and Brother Jones. They both came in together and Deacon Myers said, "I see we weren't the only ones thinking ahead." I said, "Yes, brethren, I thought it would be best to get here nice and early to set up and be able to direct the participants to their assigned seating as they arrived." Brother Jones said, "They say that great minds think alike and I'm so glad we are all on the same page."

I responded, "Well, this is the set up. The three of us will sit at the head of the table. Since I am going to be acting as the moderator, I will take the center seat, Brother Jones will be on my left, and you Deacon Myers will be seated to the right of me." Deacon Myers then asked, "Well, where are First Lady Lula, John, Matthew and Miriam going to sit?" I said, "Deacon Myers, they are going to sit to the right of you in that same order. Mark Houston and Mary Buford will sit across from them to the left of Brother Jones. Although we all will be in close proximity, unless someone jumps across the table or runs around the other end, I think we'll be in good shape." Brother Jones folded his hands in the prayer position and said, "By the grace of God, everything *will* be alright." Deacon Myers then said, "Well brothers, it's almost that time." Just as Deacon Myers uttered those words there was a knock at the door.

"Come in." I said as First Lady Lula, John, Matthew, and Miriam walked in. They all looked as if they had just been crying. Perhaps it was the larger than life portrait of Rev. Charles illuminated in the hallway that triggered their emotions. Or maybe it was the fact that they were finally going to get the answers they were so desperately searching for. Whether they had been crying or not Deacon Myers greeted them with a hardy, 'Praise the Lord' and then ushered them to their seats. As they were being seated, the air had already begun to fill with tension, especially being that they did not even respond to Deacon Myers' greeting. The looks on their faces were looks of nervous sadness and angered bewilderment.

Just as soon as they were seated, there was another knock at the door, even though it was already opened. This time, before anyone could say 'Come in' the door, already slightly ajar, was pushed opened with sort of an unfriendly force resulting in a loud noise as the door bounced off of the doorstop. It drew everyone's attention as in walked Mary Buford–Houston and Mark Houston. Mary had on large dark shades, a scarf draped over her head and wrapped around her neck and in addition to that she wore a sarcastic smirk on her face. Mark on the other hand, dressed in a suit and necktie, hesitantly walked in with his head held down and appeared to be somewhat timid. Brother Jones then said, "Come on in, and please be seated over here." As he directed them to their seats and they sat down, the tension level already high had sharply increased, resulting in a staring match. This rolling of eyes and piercing glances brought new meaning to the old phrase 'If looks could kill.'

I had to do something and quickly so I called the meeting to order and I asked Deacon Myers to open up with a word of prayer. He obliged and said, "Let us all bow our heads together in prayer. Heavenly Father, it is once more and again a few of your humble servants have gathered together in your name. Father, we have come in the name of Jesus, to discuss the business at hand. And Father God, we pray that as we take care of your business, that you would guide our tongues, guard our hearts and give us the kind of peace that passes all understanding. We ask that you bless everyone under the sound of my voice and we ask that you bless the memory of our beloved Pastor, Rev. Charles. We ask all of these things in Jesus' name and for His sake. Amen." They were scattered, soft spoken and late but I do believe that everyone uttered an 'Amen' of sorts. I then said, "Thank you, Deacon Myers for that heartfelt prayer."

As the meeting commenced, I thought it necessary to set some ground rules and establish some protocol. I opened by saying, "First of all, on behalf of Deacon Willie Myers, the Chairman of the Deacon Board, Brother Oscar Jones, the Chairman of the Trustee Board and myself, we want to thank each and everyone for your willingness to be here and participate in this rather difficult meeting. As things progress, everyone will have an opportunity to speak and be heard and we ask that no one talk over or interrupt anyone else. We ask that everyone please remain seated at all times. We also ask that you keep your voices and tones at a respectable level and please know that we cannot solve anything by shouting and or arguing. Now, I have an opening statement that will recap past and recent events and will also include some questions that will require true and honest answers. We expect everyone's full and complete cooperation in order to bring some closure and finality to this already agonizing situation."

First Lady Lula responded, "We will do our very best to maintain some decorum, but you know this is not easy for us." Then John chimed in and said, "I can't promise you that I'm going to keep my cool through all of this." I said, "Yes, I understand, but we ask that everyone please try and give it your very best effort. Now, let's look at the facts. The Green Pastures Baptist Church, in an effort to provide appropriate compensation for the serving pastor with a 25 year minimum, took out two life insurance policies for $500,000.00 each. These policies were for the Rev. Joseph M. Charles, III and upon his demise, his wife; his children and grandchildren would be the beneficiaries at his discretion, of one of the $500,000.00 policies. The other $500,000.00 policy listed the church as the sole beneficiary. Rev. Charles served well beyond the 25 year minimum and basically dedicated his entire life to Green Pastures. I'm just recalling and stating the facts, but I wanted to make sure that everyone understands and agrees. Does everyone understand what has been said thus far?" Some simply nodded while others said, "Yes, we understand."

I then asked, "Deacon Myers and Brother Jones, are the aforementioned facts correct as I have stated them? To this, they both answered, "Yes, they are correct." Then Deacon Myers said, "Please continue." I continued by saying, "It must be understood that the church paid the insurance premiums until the policies were paid in full. However, Rev. Charles had complete control over the policies and there was never any thought or consideration given to any changes being made in the beneficiaries and certainly no thought given to Rev. Charles changing the policy designated for the church over to an unnamed illegitimate son. This is where we are now and this set of circumstances has precipitated this particular meeting on today. Now I have some specific questions that are going to be directed at individuals, but I do not want anyone to feel as if this is a personal attack. This is more of an effort to get to the truth."

At this point, everyone seemed to tense up, straighten up, sit up and prepare themselves, not knowing to whom I would direct the questions first. I started with First Lady Lula. I asked, "First Lady Lula, after your husband passed away, did you and the family receive the proceeds as beneficiaries of one of the $500,000.00 life insurance policies the church had on Rev. Charles?" She answered, "We most certainly did. Everyone received exactly what Rev. Charles had designated we were to receive; me the children and the grandchildren. We didn't have any problems whatsoever." I said, "Thank you so much, First Lady." My next question was directed to Brother Jones. I said, "Brother Jones, as Chairman of the Trustee Board, what was your understanding of what the church was to receive in the event of the passing of Rev. Charles?" Brother Jones responded, "Well as far as I knew, the church paid for the policy and was expected to receive $500,000.00 as the sole beneficiary."

Then I asked, "Brother Jones, can you tell us exactly what happened when you attempted to collect on the policy?" He said, "When I called and spoke to the insurance broker and told him who I was and what my intension was, he informed me that there was some sort of major problem because the check for that policy had already been issued." I said, "What did you do then?" Brother Jones said, "I told him that I was coming right over to straighten out the whole matter." I said, "Go on, brother." He said, "When I got there, the broker told me that a young man possibly in his thirties had picked up the check because he was listed as the authorized sole beneficiary on that second policy and that he claimed to be the son of the late Rev. Charles. I asked him which son it was—John or Matthew and he said it was neither. In fact, he said that the young man's name was not to be publicized at the written request of Rev. Charles. However, the young man did have the proper identification that matched who and what was listed on the policy as beneficiary."

I said, "Brother Jones, can you give us some insight as to when the beneficiary of the policy was changed?" He responded, "I had the same question for the broker and he informed me that it was approximately ten years ago that Rev. Charles came into the office and made the request. The broker said that he didn't suspect any foul play because Rev. Charles handled all of the business concerning the policies. Although the church paid for them, all of the information and correspondence went to Rev. Charles. He signed the papers. He was the one in charge and if he desired to make any changes, he did not have to answer to anybody. He had complete power of attorney over those policies. Nevertheless, upon his death, the church did not and I repeat, did not receive any of the $500,000.00 inheritance."

I said, "Thank you Brother Jones for your input. Now, Deacon Myers can you please fill us in on the general consensus of the congregation since knowledge of this sordid tale has gotten out? Deacon Myers cleared his throat and began, "Well, to tell you the truth, there has been a whole lot of talk and a whole lot of speculation. Everyone is upset about the money issue but they are twice as upset about the adulterous affair, the illegitimate child, the lies, the deceit and the fact that Rev. Charles did not practice what he preached. The spirits of the people are broken and they are in need of healing." I said, "Deacon Myers, we want to thank you for having your hand on the pulse of the congregation and in the absence of a pastor, taking the responsibility of the spiritual leadership of this house."

The Momentum Shift

...SHE CAME TO PROVE HIM WITH THE
HARD QUESTIONS.
I KINGS 10:1B

Now, up until this point, the meeting although tension filled, was conducted rather calmly and civilly. However, that would all soon come to an end and the atmosphere would suddenly shift and take a turn for the worse. As soon as I had thanked Deacon Myers for his input, John jumped in and said, "This is all well and good but can we get down to the real nitty–gritty. I know everybody is so bent out of shape about the money and even about the infidelity because my father was the Pastor, but I believe there are some more important issues at hand. You all called this meeting and you have my mother sitting here all this time, listening to all this mess and she is cooperating; so let's stop the nonsense, stop beating around the bush and get down to the hard questions!"

As John's tone began to exude more anger, I figured I'd restore order, jump in and address Mark Houston. I said, "Brother Mark Houston, in my best efforts to assist First

Lady Lula, John, Matthew and Miriam in finding answers and closure, and in my quest to aid the church in finding out where the insurance money ended up, I began searching and digging for information that I thought would be relevant to the case. After prayerful and thoughtful consideration, I was led to question several members of the church, both past and present. I desperately needed to see if anyone could lend some assistance that would at least point me in the right direction.

So I talked with a lot of people and learned a great deal more than was intended; however each person that I had spoken with specifically recalled an altercation quite some years ago between First Lady Lula and a Mary Buford, who was the church secretary at the time. I was told that somehow First Lady Lula walked in on Rev. Charles and Mary fooling around in the Pastor's study. There was a brief struggle, Mary was fired, her membership terminated and then she relocated. Now, in my heart of hearts I felt that if this incident was etched in the minds of so many, for so many years, then there must be some sort of connection."

Mark then asked, "So what did all of that have to with me?" I answered, "At first, nothing, but as things began to unfold, I started putting the pieces together. First of all, I found your remarks rather strange at the musical and wake service for Rev. Charles. You have served on choirs under my direction for many years and have never really been vocal; and then you stand to make remarks at Rev. Charles' wake. I thought that was indeed out of the ordinary. However, what was more out of the ordinary was the content of what you said. That's what I remembered the most." Mark then asked, "You remembered what I said?" I said, "Yes, I clearly recall what you said and how you said it." Mark asked, "How I said it?" I said, "Yes, the pain and anguish in your voice ran very deep and it was unforgettable. You said and I quote, 'If I had a father, I would want my father to be just like Rev. Charles' end quote. Then a veiled mystery woman, whom most people didn't know, came and helped you back to your seat because you were on the verge of collapse. Then there was the issue of the insurance money and the mystery son. Now... I thought of the possibilities but I never told anyone because I didn't want anyone to think that I was crazy. Then I recently had a long confirming conversation with Brother Albert Best, the former Minister of Music here at Green Pastures, and he shared with me some very intimate details concerning you, and not only who your mother is but also who your father is."

Mark said, "You talked to my uncle Albert?" I said, "Yes I did and He told me everything. So, for the record, Brother Mark I need to ask you in the presence of everyone assembled, is Rev. Charles your father? Are you the mysterious son who showed up out of the blue and was in receipt of the $500,000.00 inheritance? And, is Mary Buford–Houston, who was said to be your aunt, really your biological mother?" Well, as soon as I asked Mark those questions all hell broke loose. Mark was getting ready to respond, but before he had an opportunity, there was a pounding on the table and the shrill of a loud high pitched voice of a one Mary Buford–Houston said, "Now wait just one damn minute! I am not going to sit here and allow all of you to jump all over my Mark." I said, "Excuse me ma'am, but no one is jumping all over Brother Mark. In fact, he was very calmly and very simply asked a couple of questions by me, to which *you* felt the need to jump in. As far as I can see, he is a grown man who is capable of answering for himself, if you will give him a chance." Mary then said, "Yes, he is a grown man, but you asked him a question that concerns me and I want the floor right now to answer all of your questions. I came to set the record straight!"

I said, "Alright Ms. Mary Buford–Houston, since you insist on speaking for Brother Mark, then the floor is yours." She said, "It's about time! Let me first address your questions. Mark Houston is and I repeat *is* the son of the *late* Rev. Joseph M. Charles, III. Not only is Rev. Charles Mark's biological father, but I, Mary Buford–Houston *am* Mark's mother. I am *not* his aunt. *I am his mother!* You all can sit here and judge me if you want to, but I really don't care because none of you have a heaven or a hell to put me in. First Lady Lula then said, "Mary, we are not here to judge you. We only feel that we deserve and are certainly entitled to some answers." Mary responded, "You deserve? You are entitled? What about what Mark deserves? What about the things that Mark is entitled to?" I jumped in and said, "From what I understand, first of all, you knew that Rev. Charles was a married man when you first got involved with him. Second of all, you made the choice and decision to lie and say that Mark was your nephew. Thirdly, you chose to secretly hide Mark's identity from his half siblings and from the rest of the church. Now you have the audacity to be concerned about what Mark deserves?"

Mary angrily responded, "I didn't do any of these things by myself. Neither did I make any of these decisions by myself. Don't you know that it takes two? And just for your information First Lady, I didn't get pregnant while I was still living here in New York. Your beloved Rev. Charles tracked me down. He knew that I had gotten married and he came all the way down to Alabama. Yes, he was preaching revival, but he was also laying hands on me, just like he did when you walked in on us. He came to see me after I left him. He found me and he was in love with me. Joe–Joe knew that I was pregnant with his child and he knew that I had planned on keeping the baby. He even knew of my intentions to raise Mark in New York, in Green Pastures Baptist Church. He knew that I was going to claim that Mark was my sister–in–law's child. He knew all of this and he agreed to it. I told him that I didn't want to cause any problems for him and his family but I wanted Mark to know who he was and he agreed. Yes, I conditioned Mark and told him why things had to be done this way, but that was something that I had to handle with *my* son and as he got older he understood more and more and learned to live with it. Rev. Charles and Mark had some secret visits over the years but they were few and far in between. Rev. Charles did somewhat take care of Mark financially but it was never about the money. I just wanted him to know his father. No, it has not always been easy, especially around Father's Day and around Mark's birthday, but we survived."

First Lady Lula then said, "Excuse me, Mary but you need to thank God that your son is not crazy, a crack head, or locked up in jail. Better yet, you need to thank God that he doesn't hate you for what you and Rev. Charles did to him. I'm sure he has some hidden resentment, even if he never expresses it, but you need to thank God." Miriam then shouted with tears streaming down her face, "Momma, I *know* you are not sitting here taking up for Mark?" First Lady answered, "No, it's not so much that I'm taking up for him, but the truth is that none of this is his fault." Matthew then spoke up and said, "It's not our fault either. This whole thing is just not right and every-body is acting like poor little Mark is the victim. Well, to hell with Mark! What about my poor mother and her feelings? What about our feelings?"

Mary then said, "Your poor mother knew that Rev. Charles was no good and that he was fooling around with many other women besides me. So don't sit up here talking about your poor mother! My son's feelings at this point are far more important." Well, that was the straw that broke the camel's back. Miriam lost it and went com-pletely off. Miriam, screaming at the top of her voice said, "You must be out of your damn mind, Mary Buford or Mary Houston, or whatever your name is! How in the hell are you going to sit here and disrespect not only my mother but also the memory of my deceased father! You aint no good! What about what you did in all of this? You're the home–wrecking, husband–stealing; wanna–be first lady, preacher groupie hoe, and now you and your illegitimate bastard son want to play the victim! I don't think so!"

I said, "Okay, okay, let us please remember that we are still in the house of the Lord and that we are trying to settle these matters in peace." Miriam said, "I know we are in the house of the Lord but *these* people have turned it into a den of thieves!" Mary then said, "Oh well, if that's what it is and if that's what you want to call it then, oh well!" Miriam snapped back and said, "Oh well? Oh well? I know why you keep saying 'Oh well.' You keep saying 'Oh well' because you're just like the woman at the well. Jesus blew her up and I'm about to blow you up because you've had five husbands and the one you are with right now is not your husband. Don't' think that the word isn't out on you." First Lady Lula asked, "Miriam, what are you talking about?" Miriam answered, "Momma, I've been doing some investigating of my own and I found out that daddy wasn't the only married preacher she's been with. In fact, she has been the mistress of Rev. P. J. Dixon for many years, even before his ex–wife died. And now that First Lady Dixon has passed away, she walking around strutting her stuff like she is the first lady of the Mount Moriah Baptist Church."

First Lady Lula asked, "Miriam, where did you get all of this from?" Miriam answered, "Momma, you know that Tabitha Dixon is my best friend. I needed someone to talk to about all of this stuff that we've been going through and I began confiding in her. We've been pray-ing together in the PK (Preacher's Kids) Fellowship and leaning on one another. It turns out that she also needed someone to talk with and in our exchange of stories, we figured out that both of our fathers had messed with and is currently messing with the same nasty woman, Mary Buford." Mary then said, "Whatever! This has nothing to do with why we are here today and for the record, once again, I don't give a damn what you all say or think about me. Right now, it's about my son and making sure he gets everything he's entitled to. What Joe–Joe did with the insurance policy was all his doing. He told Mark about it a few years ago but we had nothing to do with it. We didn't even believe him. To tell you the truth, I don't know why he did it. Maybe he was motivated by guilt because of the circumstances. Whatever the case, Mark received that money legally and to me it's really just a down payment on all that he has missed out on. Now everything is out in the open. Everybody knows that Rev. Charles *is* Mark's father and I am his mother. Everybody knows that Mark is the one who received the inheritance and as far as I am concerned, this meeting is adjourned. Come on Mark; let's get the hell out of here!"

At the moment, John stood up and said, "Wait a minute. Wait a minute. Before you go, I just want to say one more thing to you Mark. Yes, there is some anger and resentment, some misunderstanding and some pain, but the fact remains... Mark, you are our brother. You've been our brother in Christ all of your life before we knew that you were our biological brother. And if you will allow us some time to heal and some time to process all of this, maybe we can have some sort of sibling relationship in the future." Miriam just sucked her teeth and then Matthew said, "That's going to take more than some time. It's going to take a miracle." Mark stood up to extend his hand to John in agreement and in an instant Mary snatched him by the hand and they exited the room.

An Inside Job

A BASTARD SHALL NOT ENTER INTO THE CONGREGATION
OF THE LORD...
DEUTERONOMY 23:2

After Mark and Mary's abrupt exit, the meeting at that point was pretty much over. However, we did close in prayer. Brother Jones offered a soul stirring prayer and he prayed for all who were in attendance including those who had made an early departure. Deacon Myers and Brothers Jones both stated that they were each going to their respective homes. At the request of First Lady Lula; I went along with her, John, Matthew and Miriam to the Charles residence. This was an impromptu meeting, I guess to discuss what had transpired at the meeting we just had. With all that had come out, I could see that the entire family was not only in a great deal of pain and disbelief but they also looked like deer caught in the headlights.

We all pulled up to the house at the same time and then got out of our cars. It was slow and methodical walk to the front door. Somehow everyone had managed to throw their arms around someone else and we basically hugged our way up to the house. John and First Lady Lula were clinging to each other and I was in the middle of Matthew and Miriam. We were all holding and supporting each other. When we got in the house, First Lady Lula said, "Now listen here, we're not going to be sitting up here all night, but I want to talk a little bit about what happened at the meeting. I'm going to put on some tea for me and some hot chocolate, because I know you all don't want any tea. Miriam, you look in the kitchen cabinet and get those shortbread cookies and bring them into the den." Miriam answered, "Yes ma'am." Then Matthew added, "Miriam, please bring the marshmallows too. I can't have my hot chocolate without marshmallows."

With everyone sipping and chewing and comfortably nestled in the family rooms chairs, the dialogue would now begin. First Lady Lula started off by asking, "Is everyone okay? I know it was a lot to swallow all in one sitting, but if you have anything to say or if you want to vent, then the time is right now. None of you need to lay down tonight without having the chance to say what you are feeling about what's really going on in your head and your heart." There was a brief moment of silence and then Miriam broke down and cried out, "Why momma? Why would daddy allow his illegitimate son to be raised up right alongside of us in the church? Why?" As she wiped away the tears from her eyes, First Lady Lula said, "Baby girl, I wish I could answer your question, but that's a question that only your father could have answered." First Lady looked up toward heaven and said, "Lord Jesus, give me strength! Miriam, I can't believe it myself and I don't understand how he could have carried that kind of secret for so many years. I imagine your father must have been in a terrible amount of pain. Any man who was not able to love and cherish his own flesh and blood freely and openly must have been in excruciating pain."

Matthew asked, "Momma, are you trying to get us to feel sorry for daddy? Are you trying to get us to have some compassion for this man who not only cheated on you repeatedly, but also had the nerve to subject us to growing up as friends with a kid that turned out to be our half brother? He needed to be in some pain because he should have been man enough to come forward and admit his mistakes. His whole life as this great pastor, leader and man of fidelity and truth was a complete lie. It's funny because everybody got so angry with me way back then when I said that my father wasn't there for me because he was too busy being daddy to everybody else. Well, damn it! He really was being daddy but it wasn't to everybody else. It was for his little bastard son." Matthew breaks down and begins to weep aloud. First Lady Lula caresses his back and then says, "Matthew, I understand your frustrations. Go ahead and let them out, but be careful that you are not too hard on him." Matthew replies through his tears with his voice cracking, "Too hard on him? Me, be too hard on him? Momma, when I think about how hard he came down on me when I had my problems and was on drugs, lying and stealing. When I think about the degrading and demoralizing things that this man said to me and the names he called me, I can't help but think that he never said anything like that to Mark. And Mark, his little angel, was just as big a liar as he was because he knew that daddy was his father too."

John then says, "Mark knew that daddy was his father, but you have to remember that he was programmed, brainwashed by his mother from as early as he could remember to know that our daddy was his father too but he could never acknowledge it." Matthew then says, "So is that our problem? Hell no! It is not our problem and I don't care what you say, I do not want a relationship with Mark Houston. Your little speech at the meeting was noble and good fodder for talk show ratings, but in this life it is not going to happen. I have one brother and one sister and that's it." John responded, "Matthew, whether you accept it or not, you have another brother who has the same blood running through his veins that you have running through yours. Hating him is not going to bring daddy back or change the facts."

Matthew then says, "Oh, so I guess you're okay with the fact that this little bastard profited $400,000.00 more from the insurance policy than we did as a result of *our* daddy's death?" John answered, "No. I'm not okay with it because technically that money belonged to the church. But Matthew, if you really look at it, that money that Mark received, nowhere near pays for the love, attention and affection that he missed out on." Matthew again responds, "You're right, John. That money cannot replace the love and affection that little Marky Mark missed out on, but after daddy died, little Mark the victim, didn't waste any time in going to collect. He could have alerted us a long time ago that he was our brother. When he came of age, he had to have realized that this whole thing wasn't right. Even if daddy didn't have the guts to tell us himself, Mark was around us all the time and he could have told us. Don't you see something wrong with that, John?" John said, "I'm not saying its right, but what I am trying to get you to see is that your healing will not take place as long as you have that anger, hatred and malice in your heart." Matthew then says, "Well Bro, that's just something that

. I have to work out between me and Jesus. Yawl pray for me, you hear. "

John then says, "I don't want you to think that I'm not impacted by this experience. I am. I am angry and I am hurting very deeply just like everybody else, but we have to keep on living. In order for us to keep on living we must learn to forgive. Our healing is going to be predicated on whether or not we are able to forgive. I'm not saying that tomorrow we have to invite Mark to come and live with us and spend every waking moment with us. However, we cannot ignore the fact that the one thing we have in common with Mark is our father. This man is our brother. The sooner we come to grips with that, the better off we will all be."

Then Miriam asked, "What about momma? Nobody is going through right now more than momma. Who is going to help momma heal? John answered, "Aside from the grace and mercy of God, little sister, we are. We are going to help momma. Do you not understand that momma really has no connection to Mark, but if we extend our love to Mark and are open to a relationship with him, that will further validate the love and caring that momma has instilled in us. That will help momma." First Lady Lula then said, "Listen, I want you all to hear me real good. I'm going to be just fine. What I have dealt with over the years has pretty much prepared me for any and everything. Although this is the first incident of an outside child or should I say an inside child, that I know of, to me it was par for the course. So children, don't worry about me. God has given me peace. My prayer now is that you will all find peace and forgiveness in your hearts. Forgive your father and show love to your father's son."

As you can see, for much of that conversation and

exchange, I said nothing. I shed some tears throughout, but I spoke no words. Although I wanted to, because I felt as if I was part of the family; it was important for them to have this dialogue without the input of a non–family member. I was just privileged and blessed to be in the midst for the beginning of their healing process. The Bible says in Ecclesiastes 3:1... To every thing there is a season, and a time to every purpose under the heaven. Then down in verse 7 it says... a time to keep silence and a time to speak... Choose your time wisely.

THE BITTER PILL

NOW WHEN THE CONGREGATION WAS BROKEN UP... PAUL
AND BARNABAS: WHO, SPEAKING TO THEM,
PERSUADED THEM TO CONTINUE IN THE GRACE OF GOD.
ACTS 13:43

News of the big meeting on Saturday, October 21, 2002 at 1:00 PM, with all of the involved parties was common knowledge and so naturally the entire congregation was awaiting the outcome. I had spoken with Deacon Myers and suggested to him that he waste no time in meeting with the church and informing them of only the necessary and pertinent facts concerning the insurance money and the mystery child. He agreed and the very next day, October 22, 2002, as Chairman of the Deacon Board, he would call an emergency meeting immediately after the 11:00 morning worship service. So, the church clerk read the church announcements, she ended in her usual way by saying, "Please remember to call, visit or send cards to our sick and shut–in and govern yourselves accordingly to all of our announcements. We will have a special announcement at this time coming from Deacon Myers."

Deacon Myers makes his way up to the podium, adjusts the microphone, and then says, "Praise the Lord. Brothers and sisters, members of Green Pastures, immediately following this morning's worship services we will have an emergency meeting. It is business of importance and it is for adult members only. Deacons and ushers will make sure that all non–members and children promptly exit the sanctuary and then the meeting will commence. The children can wait in the fellowship hall. I'm asking all youth leaders to assist in that area. Thank you for your cooperation." As I surveyed the sanctuary from my perch on the organ, I noticed that Mark Houston was in attendance, but as I looked for the Charles family, I could only find First Lady Lula and Miriam. Evidently, John and Matthew had both decided to take a Sunday off. I really don't think they would have, had they known that there would be a called meeting today.

Not surprisingly, the church was just about full. The membership definitely had an attitude of expectancy because 11:00 AM worship service, although usually well attended, was uncharacteristically running over. Not only was the overflow area filled to capacity, but the ushers also had extra chairs down the aisles. Somebody came to find out something. Nevertheless, after the benediction was given, the usual exuberant fellowship and joyful greeting was curtailed. The Deacons and ushers were immediately on their posts making sure that all of the non–members and children were escorted from the sanctuary. When it was determined that the house was in order and that all who remained were in fact members, Deacon Myers called the meeting to order.

He again strolled up to the microphone and said, "This emergency meeting of the membership of the

Green Pastures Baptist Church is called to order. Today's date is Sunday, October 22, 2002, and the time is 2:35 PM. This is not a question and answer forum. I repeat. The floor will not be opened today for a question and answer period. However, at another time in the very near future, we will schedule another meeting where you *will* be able to ask questions. Today's meeting is just an informational meeting. Some things have transpired, some discoveries have been made and in an attempt to quell all of the extra talk, Brother Oscar Jones, the Chairman of the Trustees and me thought it would be in the best interest of the church that we inform you of what has taken place."

As Deacon Myers was speaking, I began to look around again. This time since service was over; I sat in the front row where the deacons normally sit. First Lady Lula and Miriam were sitting right behind me. Mark was on the other side seated about middle way of the sanctuary in the left center aisle. Deacon Myers continued, "I am not going to prolong the time by rehashing everything that has already happened, but I will give a brief statement so that everyone is on the same page. As most of you now, the church was supposed to receive $500,000.00 from one of the life insurance policies of the late Rev. Joseph M. Charles, III. The church paid for the policies however, Rev. Charles over the years had full control over the policies with no interference or objection from the church. The reason the church trusted Rev. Charles to handle that business was because there were two policies; one for his family and one for the church. There was no reason to suspect that Rev. Charles would mishandle or change anything regarding the policies. However, that was not the case."

The congregation began to buzz with excitement

because they knew that the answers they had been waiting for were finally here. Deacon Myers continued, "Well, about ten years ago, Rev. Charles legally changed the beneficiary on the policy that was supposed to be for the church. What was supposed to be left to the church, we later found out was left to a young man who turned out to be the illegitimate son and I say that with no disrespect, the illegitimate son of the late Rev. Charles. We have consulted with the church's lawyer, and legally there is nothing we can do, because Rev. Charles who was an authorized signatory had full power of attorney over those policies, even though the church paid for them." At that moment a wind of hostility had begun to blow throughout the church and you could hear the murmurings."

Deacon Myers continued and said, "In searching out the legal ramifications, we were also looking to identify this mystery son. And brothers and sisters, this is perhaps the most difficult part right here. We have since found out that Rev. Charles' son, who collected the insurance money, is one among us." With that statement, the buzz quickly turned into a dull roar. The sanctuary was filled with random questions being asked aloud. The questions of, "What, who is it, what's his name?" now filled the air. Deacon Myers responded and shouted, "Order! Let us come to order in the sanctuary." At his request the people began to simmer down. Deacon Myers continued, "We have discovered that our very own Brother Mark Houston is the son of the late Rev. Charles. Not only, but his mother is Ms. Mary Buford–Houston, who was one of our past members that was excommunicated because of a social conflict of interest. And judging from the current situation at hand, we can surmise what the social conflict of interest was."

Just then, as if it were in slow motion, the entire congregation all turned their heads and focused their eyes directly on Brother Mark Houston, who just sat there with tears rolling down his face. One of the ushers brought him some tissues and he wiped his eyes and then buried his face into his hands. Deacon Myers then said, "This has been an extremely challenging ordeal for all of us, but let us not bombard Brother Mark with all kinds of questions. Nobody knows what he has had to go through all of these years. Let us have some compassion on him. Also, let us keep in mind that in addition to still healing from the loss of Rev. Charles, First Lady Lula, John, Matthew and Miriam and the rest of the family now have a whole new set of issues that they must contend with. I appeal to each and every one of you, I implore you, I beg of you to please not bother First Lady Lula and the family. Pray for them. Send them a card of encouragement but please do not call them, question them, talk about them, or disgrace the memory of Rev. Charles."

When Deacon Myers asked the congregation not to disgrace the memory of Rev. Charles, there suddenly arose another buzz with people talking among themselves and murmuring. Without actually hearing what was being said throughout the congregation, the overall feeling was that Rev. Charles' own secrets and lies had already disgraced his memory. Deacon Myers, once again called the house to order by saying, "Let us please stop talking amongst ourselves and prepare to close in prayer. Please be mindful of all that has been said and I'm asking everyone to continue to pray concerning these matters and most of all for the Green Pastures Baptist Church. Let us pray. Dear Lord, dismiss us from this place but never from thy presence. These and all prayers we ask in Jesus' name, Amen."

Most people did say 'Amen' but they went right from 'Amen' to talking about the devastating things they had just learned. Some people were actually crying, while others were huddled together in prayer. Still others were showing signs of anger and disgust. As I continued to assess things, I could see a few people gathered around Mark Houston, extending their hands and even hugging him as he made his way out of the church. First Lady Lula and Miriam were also surrounded by supporters and busybody reporters. Embraces, kisses and hand shakes also impeded their exit. But they were gracious and did not cut anyone short. Their strength in the face of this kind of adversity was indeed a blessing to all. This bitter pill was a horse pill and everyone was forced to swallow it straight with no chaser.

DADDY NEVER ACKNOWLEDGED

WHILE THE PHARISEES WERE GATHERED TOGETHER,
JESUS ASKED THEM, SAYING, WHAT THINK YE OF CHRIST?
WHOSE SON IS HE?
MATTHEW 22:41–42A

Deacon Myers, Brother Jones and I were standing in the parking lot of the church conversing, when all of a sudden one of the brethren approached and asked us a question. His name was Dr. Leroy King. Dr. King was a longtime member of Green Pastures as well as a very prominent and well respected pediatrician in the community. Practically all of the children in the church were patients of his; as were most of their parents. He said to the three of us, "Excuse me, but may I ask a question that has been plaguing my mind. I heard you say in the meeting that, along with the church attorney, you searched out the legality of the changing of the beneficiary and the legality of the insurance company releasing the $500,000.00 to one Mr. Mark Houston, the newly discovered son of the late Rev. Charles. I also heard you say that legally everything seemed to be in order and that the insurance company would not have released the check if the law had been broken. My question is this. Has it ever been conclusively proven that Mark Houston is actually the biological son of Rev. Charles? You know we live in a day and time where, if I may use the term 'baby mama drama,' is part of our every day experience. You cannot turn on the television without one of the daytime talk show episodes being devoted to issues of paternity."

Wow! Dr. King's question sent a high–frequency shock wave among the three of us. We all stretched our eyes, looked at each other, shook our heads and threw up our hands as if to say, we never even considered the remote possibility that paternity had never officially been established. Why? Why was that? With the stakes so high and the potential for eminent disaster so evident, why wasn't the question of paternity discussed at all. Was it because we were so *driven* to find out who the mystery child was? Was it because we had tunnel vision, or blinders on, focusing squarely on finding out who the mother was? Did it have something to do with the fact that this was a reverend, who although he had messed up, was trying to make restitution by financially enhancing the life of the son whom he had never publicly acknowledged? After all, this woman, the mother, Mary Buford–Houston, knew that Rev. Charles was a married man and obviously wasn't concerned much about her reputation. Her morals and scruples were pretty much nonexistent. So, did Rev. Charles take *her* word that the child was his? And does that mean that we had to take her word also?

Well, to answer Dr. King's question I said to him, "To be honest, doctor, I'm not sure if conclusive evidence of proof of paternity has been established; at least, not that we have seen. This son in question is approximately

35 years old and I don't know what kind of procedures they had done back then to prove paternity, but as far as this recent discovery is concerned, I know that no such modern procedure has been done. Listen. We don't even know if Rev. Charles' name is on Mark's birth certificate because we have never seen a birth certificate either. It was a complete oversight due in part to the fact that we could not possibly believe that Rev. Charles would bequeath $500,000.00 to a young man if he was not 100 percent sure he was the father. Forgive me for saying this doctor but Mary really put it on Rev. Charles and had his nose wide open. It's no telling if he even inquired about it himself. On the other hand, maybe Rev. Charles knew that the baby was his. He did have some prior fatherly experience and Mark does look a little bit like him. At this juncture it is definitely something that we must look into." Dr. King then said, "Well, I don't know if any good will come of it, but it is worth the time and consideration. I suggest that you and the attorney look into it at once." I replied, "We most certainly will."

At this point, we bid each other farewell and departed to our several destinations with plenty on our minds. I thought to myself, just when I began to think that things were starting to quiet down and mellow out; here comes the doctor. This question that the doctor has asked presented us with an entirely new set of circumstances. How were we going to find out whether or not paternity has ever been established and who were we going to ask. Should we ask Mark or would we have to deal with Mary all over again? If it turned our that Rev. Charles was not Mark Houston's biological father, would it have any bearing at this point on the legality of the insurance money transaction? I took me some time to gather all of my thoughts and set a plan in motion. However, I knew that time was of the essence.

I made up my mind to start with Mark first because I reasoned that if he *had* the answers that I was seeking, then I would not have to even deal with the somewhat outlandish often combative Mary Buford–Houston. On the other hand, if Mark did not possess the satisfactory answers concerning proof of paternity, he would at least be the only connection we had to his mother, Mary. The next day in the evening, which was that Monday after the big meeting at the church, I called Mark on the telephone. He said, "Hello, Mark speaking." I said, "Hey there Brother Mark." He then said, "Hello. To what do I owe *this* call? Is there something else wrong?" I said, "No. There is nothing wrong. I just need to speak with you brother to brother and I would rather we not do it on the telephone." He said, "Does it have to do with everything that's going on? I said, "Yes, but hopefully things will soon get back to normal." He said to me, "Believe me when I tell you. Things will *never* be normal again."

I said as I chuckled, "You know what, man? You might be right about that? That, however, doesn't stop us from going on with our lives, now does it?" He said, "I'm trying. I'm really trying. When and where do you want to meet?" I told him, "Let's get together tomorrow evening around 6:30 pm at my place." He said, "Can we make it a little bit later than that? I have a class tomorrow that doesn't let out until 8:00." I answered, "Yes, it can be later. How about 8:30. Can you get to my house by 8:30? He said, "Yes, I'm only coming from across the bridge in Manhattan." I said, "Mark, I didn't know you were in school. What are you going for?" Mark answered, "Well, I finished up my undergrad work and now I'm working on my Masters of

Divinity over at Allegiance Theological Seminary. This is my last class and then I will be official." I said, "Mark, I didn't know you were interested in ministry." Mark answered, "Well, I haven't preached my initial sermon yet but I've been teaching Sunday School at church for about six years now. Ministry and church is all I know. It is my whole life. I have been studying and preparing for quite some time and I wanted to make sure that when I finally came out, I came out fully credentialed, just like… my father did."

I said, "That's great news and I'm really happy for you. I'll see you tomorrow at my house at around 8:30 and we'll be able to talk some more. He said, "Alright, I'll see you then. You have a good night." He hung up the telephone but I didn't move because I was in a state of suspended animation. I just sat there with the phone in my hand and my mouth wide open. I was absolutely flabbergasted, dumbfounded, befuddled and astonished. Who knew, that Mark Houston, the one whom we just found out was the illegitimate son of the late Rev. Charles, was pursuing a career in ministry? Does it get any better than that? He was secretly following in his father's footsteps. The same father who never acknowledged him, yet he loved and respected this man and what he stood for so much that he still wanted to emulate him. Mark, knowing Rev. Charles was his father from his youth, seeing this man on at least a weekly basis all of his life, knowing his marital and family status, interacting with his half–siblings, watching them receive the royal treatment because they were the first family, still wanted to be just like his daddy and his daddy never acknowledged him. Just in case you missed it in the title of this chapter, Daddy Never Acknowledged.

I was so looking forward to talking more with Mark

that I could hardly wait for the next day to get here. When the next day came, I went through the day being preoccupied with yesterday's conversation and the anticipation of today's conversation. I must admit also that Mark's pursuit of ministry aspirations, in spite of everything, has caused me to feel a great deal of sympathy and compassion toward him. It was getting close to our meeting time and as I was fixing up a little snack tray the doorbell rang. I went to get the door and it was indeed Mark. As I opened the door and let him in, I said, "Please come in and make yourself at home." He said, "Thank you. Man, this is a nice place." As he walked around and looked at a few pictures, he made his way over to my music room and said, Oh! I see you have a B3 Hammond Organ and a Baby Grand Piano in your music room." I said, "Yeah, I can't live without those." He said, "I know this building must be rocking." I said, "Yes, but sometimes my neighbors complain. Come on into the living room and sit down so we can talk."

Mark then made his way into the living room and we sat down. I said, "I have some snacks here and some iced tea. Help yourself and don't be shy." Mark said, "You don't have to worry about that, as hungry as I am. What did you want to talk about anyway, that we could not talk about over the telephone?" I hesitated at first but then I answered, "Well... I know this entire ordeal has been rather stressful for you but another issue has come up and I figured that I should talk with you first." He said, "What issue? What else is there?" I responded, "The issue of proof of paternity has arisen. It has been brought up as a possible rebuttal to legality of you receiving the insurance money instead of the church." Mark responded, "Rev. Charles is my father. I have not always been able to say that openly or publicly, but now I can because I know beyond a shadow of doubt that he is my father."

I said, "Mark, that's not the issue here. The issue is whether or not it has been legally established that Rev. Joseph M. Charles, III is your father. Do you have your birth certificate or a copy of your birth certificate listing Rev. Charles as the father with his signature on it?" Mark answered, "Yes. I have my original birth certificate with my father's name and signature on it. In addition to that, about ten years ago I was also given by my mother, a copy of the results of a paternal blood test, taken back in 1977, that conclusively declared the Rev. Joseph M. Charles, III as the biological father of Mark Anthony Houston. Whoever needs to see them, I will furnish them upon request." I said, "Brother Mark, I'm satisfied with that and as long as those legal documents are in order nobody can say anything. The birth certificate and the results of a blood test taken back in 1977 are proof enough for me, but there are going to be some naysayers like Dr. Leroy King, who will bring up the more accurate and more recent phenomenon of deoxyribonucleic acid, better known as DNA."

Mark then said, "They can bring up DNA all they want to, it really doesn't matter. I've already done the homework and the birth certificate and results of the prior test will stand up in any court of law. So, whoever it is, tell them to bring it on." With that statement, I figured that this meeting was now over and I said to Mark, "Well, I thank you for your time and for being so open and honest with me. Since you have been so honest with me, I will share with you that it was about ten years ago that Rev. Charles changed the insurance policy and made you beneficiary. The reason I'm telling you that is because it coincides with what you just told me. Although the blood test was taken back in 1977, you said it was also about ten years ago that your mother presented the results to you. That leads me to believe that your mother gave you and Rev. Charles those test results at the same time, and then Rev. Charles for what ever reason went and changed the policy." Mark said, "Thank you for that bit of information but I already knew that. My mother and my father were both very forthcoming with me. Listen, I'll talk to you at another time. And again, any information needed, please call me and let me know. Take care." As Mark walked out of the door we shook hands, embraced and I said to him, "Get home safely."

The New Beginning...

SO THE LAST SHALL BE FIRST, AND THE FIRST LAST...
MATTHEW 20:16A

After meeting with Mark, I found out that he preemptively sent copies of his birth certificate and the results of the paternal blood test, both proving that Rev. Charles was his father, to Deacon Myers, Brother Jones, Dr. King, First Lady Lula, the insurance company and the attorney for Green Pastures. Not only did he send them, but he sent them in triplicate. It was a bold initiative on his part but it certainly quieted the rabble–rousers who had begun stirring up trouble concerning the issue of paternity along with the legality of the changing of the insurance policy. I was beginning to realize that Mark was a lot smarter and a bit more industrious than most people gave him credit for being.

Along with Mark's birth certificate and blood test results was a letter. This letter, addressed to the officers and members of Green Pastures Baptist Church, stated that as a tithe paying member in good standing of the Green Pastures Baptist Church, he would *temporarily* be worshipping over at the Mount Moriah Baptist Church under the leadership of Rev. P. J. Dixon for a three month period. He also made sure that he informed them that although he would be worshipping at Mount Moriah, he would still be paying his tithe at Green Pastures. You do remember the connection, don't you? Mount Moriah is the church that Mark's mother, Mary Buford–Houston belongs to and is practically the first lady, because of her *longtime* relationship with the *recent* widower, Rev. Dixon.

Both Green Pastures and Mount Moriah belong to the NBA which is the Northeastern Baptist Association. Because Green Pastures doesn't have a pastor, the Northeastern Baptist Association which is affiliated with the Allegiance Theological Seminary, which is where Mark is getting his Masters of Divinity from, had assigned him to deliver his initial sermon and do his internship over at the Mount Moriah Baptist Church. Upon the completion of his internship and on the job training under Rev. Dixon, Mark would then return to Green Pastures either as a serving minister, as interim pastor or even as pastor elect under the discretion of the moderator of the NBA and with the approval of the pulpit committee. If things were to transpire in this manner it would certainly be the ultimate vindication for the one who has suffered the most. I mean, if we were to really examine all of the persons involved in this saga, Mark undoubtedly suffered the most. And the sad part is that he suffered at the hands of both his mother and his father.

Things were pretty subdued during the three month period that Mark was away from Green Pastures fulfilling his internship. Yes, people were still talking among themselves about Mark being Rev. Charles' son and how he was secretly raised in the church, but Mark was generally a good guy and very active in the church and most people liked him. In the beginning everyone was upset over the money but the whole issue of the money had all but faded away and everyone's attention was now focused on moving on from this point.

The first anniversary of Rev. Charles' passing also occurred during this time. As you know, Rev. Charles passed away on January 17, 2002. So when January 17, 2003 rolled around, it officially ended the one year period of mourning. On that day there was a memorial service scheduled to commemorate the one year of his passing as well as remove the purple and black bunting from the facade of the church and unveil his pulpit chair. The service started promptly at 7:00 PM, the time for which it was scheduled.

There was a beautiful portrait of a robed Rev. Charles on an easel standing in front of the pulpit. Directly alongside of it was another easel with a collage of pictures dating all the way back to Rev. Charles' early years up to his most recent and last years. Needless to say, there was a constant stream of onlookers viewing the reminiscent collage. As the service began, everyone was asked to be seated. First Lady Lula, John and his family, Matthew and his family, and Miriam and her son were all seated at the front of the nearly packed sanctuary. They were all dressed immaculately and once again exemplified the epitome of class and dignity. Even after being under the inclusive swirling cloud of gossip and speculation for almost a year, they emerged at the memorial with their heads held high, not giving any place to the negativity surrounding the misdeeds of Rev. Charles. The focus was not to be on the mistakes or the sins of Rev. Charles. The purpose of this memorial was to focus strictly on the socioeconomic impact he had made in the community due to the many programs he had begun, as well as the ecclesiastical accomplishments he had made that enhanced the overall ministry.

During the memorial service, Deacon Myers informed the church that as a result of this memorial service, the removal of the bunting and unveiling of the pulpit chair, Green Pastures would form a pulpit committee and the search for a new pastor would begin ASAP. In addition to that, he also informed all in attendance that a request had been made to the Mayor of the City of New York, the Brooklyn Borough President, and other elected officials, that a portion of the street where Green Pastures stood, be renamed as a monument for his 46 years of community service, The Rev. Joseph M. Charles, III Boulevard. When Deacon Myers revealed to the church that the request had been granted for the renaming of the street; the congregation exploded in an exuberant expression of praise and a standing ovation that lasted for approximately ten minutes. After the thunderous ovation, everyone joined in and sang 'Precious Memories' and the benediction was given.

Mark…he was at the memorial service but he intentionally kept a low profile in an effort not to cause any unwanted distractions or disruptions. There were a few unscrupulous people who had sought him out and asked him some inappropriate personal questions about the money and about his relationship with his siblings, but he did not entertain them and managed to get away from there without incident. Mark had his head on straight and his focus was on bigger and better things. He had a plan that was already set in motion and he would not let anyone or anything get in the way of what he believed was God's will for his life.

The truth is that he was an exceptional young man. With all that he had endured, with all that he had been through, he could have ended up just another little black boy who had chosen the wrong path. He could have ended up just another number in a world of negative statistics. This was a young man whose mother convinced him that it was okay for him to grow up with everyone thinking that she was his aunt and that his real mother was strung out on drugs and had abandoned him. She made him think that it was okay for him to be raised in church watching his father the Pastor, openly love and interact with his half siblings and yet publicly neglect and ignore him. She made him believe that it was okay to keep his true identity secret throughout his entire life, even into adulthood. She made this boy live a lie for his entire life all under the auspices of spiritual truth and everything that the church stands for.

Mark's determination to excel despite his potentially mind destroying, sanity assassinating, ego crushing, self esteem deflating maltreatment, is a testimony of God's grace, mercy and unconditional love. This same grace, mercy and love allowed Mark, after reaching an age of maturity, accountability and responsibility, to still love and honor both his mother and his father. Both his mother and his father provoked him to anger and to wrath and yet he never disrespected either of them. With just cause and reason to do otherwise, he still exercised the discipline and obedience necessary to please God and in the end he defended their honor. I loved Rev. Charles. I still love First Lady Lula, John, Matthew, and Miriam, but the more I get to know Mark and analyze everything that he's been through, the more I love and respect him. Mark had made an indelible *'mark'* on me.

Evidently, I was not the only one whom Mark had made an unforgettable mark on. The majority of the thirteen members on the newly formed pulpit committee of Green Pastures turned out to be strong supporters of Mark Houston. Several impressive resumes came across the desks of the committee, but none were given the consideration that Mark's was. In fact, the committee was stacked with quite a few individuals that grew up with Mark right in Green Pastures. So Mark, having now preached his initial sermon, and having finished his internship over at Mount Moriah, was unanimously selected by the pulpit committee as the sole candidate for Pastor of the Green Pastures Baptist Church. In a called church meeting that was overseen by the moderator of the Northeastern Baptist Association, Mark Houston was presented as the lone candidate for the Pastoral position. The moderator's experience and influence helped to steer the congregation not to waste any more precious time and get this young man, who is familiar with the structure and the inner workings of the church already, into place. And just like that, Minister Mark A. Houston, the illegitimate son of the former Pastor, was voted in as Pastor–Elect of the Green Pastures Baptist Church. He officially began serving on the first Sunday in April 2003.

This Pastoral appointment would soon be solidified with the Ordination Services for Minister Mark A. Houston followed by the Installation Services. However, prior to both of the services, Minister Mark A. Houston procured the services of a civil attorney to assist him in legally changing his last name from Houston, to that of his father's, Charles. This process would take about a month but be completed in plenty of time so that when the actual services took place in September; the newly elected Pastor would be ordained and installed as Rev. Mark A. Charles, the son of the late Rev. Joseph M. Charles, III.

There were so many great things happening in the life of the former Brother Mark Houston, that it seemed almost too good to be true. In addition to his new appointment, in June of 2003, the now Pastor–Elect Mark A. Charles announced his engagement to his long-time girlfriend, Ms. Abigail Rebecca Coleman. This was sort of a fairytale match made in heaven because Abigail was the foster daughter of Mr. and Mrs. Thaddeus and Leona Coleman. The Colemans were longtime members of Green Pastures also who had no children of their own. They rescued Abigail from a very abusive situation and later adopted her. Mark and Abigail were best friends all throughout their school years and took their friendship to another level about seven years ago.

I guess by now you are wondering what happened to First Lady Lula, John, Matthew and Miriam. Well, First Lady Lula knew that it was time for a changing of the guard. With the appointment of Pastor–Elect Mark A. Charles and the announcement of his engagement, Lula Mae Charles would no longer be First Lady. She decided to relocate down to Alpharetta, Georgia and she took Miriam and her son with her. Not wanting to be far away from their mother, John and his family soon followed and settled in Stone Mountain, Georgia. Matthew and his family were next and they ended up in Atlanta, Georgia. They all came back to Brooklyn, New York to Green Pastures, for Pastor Mark and Lady Abigail's wedding. In fact, John and Matthew were Mark's best men and Miriam was Abigail's maid of honor. After the wedding, however, they all returned to their beautiful new homes in Georgia and continued to make new lives for themselves.

You are probably also wondering what happened to Mary Buford–Houston. Well, Mary finally got her wish.

Rev. P. J. Dixon after receiving many ultimatums broke down and proposed to Mary. They were married and she officially became First Lady Mary Dixon, the *second, first* lady of the Mount Moriah Baptist Church. As for me... well, I just play this here organ...

EPILOGUE

There is a consumer warning that suggests that the buyer beware. This warning is intended to alert the buyer to the fact that there might be a defect in the purchased product or an invisible or hidden flaw not so easily recognizable at first. However, it will subsequently manifest and perhaps render the product inoperable or of non–effect.

Well, in the spirit realm, this book was written as a Kingdom warning that suggests that the believer beware. Everything in Christendom is not always as it appears. That is why God has gifted us with the ability to discern and try the Spirit by the Spirit, to see if it is of God. I'm sure there are a plethora of Christian experiences that are book worthy, but not many are willing to share them. If believers know what to watch out for then they become more powerful in the Kingdom. I wrote this story so that ultimately God is gloried, believers are edified, and the devil is horrified. In the end, God has the final word and here it is:

11. *And He gave some, apostles; and some, prophets; and some, evangelists; and some, pastors and teachers;*

12. *For the perfecting of the saints, for the work of the ministry, for the edifying of the body of Christ:*

13. *Till we all come in the unity of the faith, and of the knowledge of the Son of God, unto a perfect man, unto the measure of the stature of the fullness of Christ:*

14. *That we henceforth be no more children, tossed to and fro, and carried about with every wind of doctrine, by the sleight of men, and cunning craftiness, whereby they lie in wait to deceive;*

15. *But speaking the truth in love, may grow up into Him in all things, which is the head, even Christ: Ephesians 4:11–15*